Robert C. Barratt

Long Life and Peace

memorials of Mrs. Elizabeth Shaw - for eighty-seven years a member of the

Wesleyan-Methodist Church

Robert C. Barratt

Long Life and Peace
memorials of Mrs. Elizabeth Shaw - for eighty-seven years a member of the Wesleyan-Methodist Church

ISBN/EAN: 9783337223953

Printed in Europe, USA, Canada, Australia, Japan

Cover: Foto ©Raphael Reischuk / pixelio.de

More available books at **www.hansebooks.com**

"LONG LIFE AND PEACE:"

MEMORIALS

OF

MRS. ELIZABETH SHAW,

FOR EIGHTY-SEVEN YEARS A
MEMBER OF THE WESLEYAN-METHODIST CHURCH.

BY

ROBERT C. BARRATT.

LONDON:
WESLEYAN CONFERENCE OFFICE
2, CASTLE STREET, CITY ROAD;
SOLD AT 66, PATERNOSTER ROW.

1875.

To the Glory of God;

And with the hope of encouraging Christians in the midst of life's trials to continue their journey heavenward, as well as of leading some young readers to consecrate their early days to the Lord, I have briefly traced the life-history of "a mother in Israel," who feared God from her youth up, whose memory is precious, and whose example ought not to be forgotten.

May He in Whom she trusted, and Whose faithfulness she proved during an unusually lengthened pilgrimage, vouchsafe His blessing.

CONTENTS.

CHAPTER I.

CHAPTER XIV.

CHAPTER XV.

MEMORIALS

OF

MRS. ELIZABETH SHAW.

———◆———

CHAPTER I.

"LITTLE BETSEY."

THESE manuscripts! what shall we do with them? On the oldest Time has already made its mark. The first pages were written by a godly maiden some eighty years ago; the last by a saintly matron when her long life was well-nigh ended. They were not meant for the public eye. Believing that a journal would prove helpful to her in her Christian course, she wrote one. She had no other end in view; and doubtless that end was answered. But is there not in these closely-written volumes much that is calculated to interest and

B

benefit all who are travellers in the road she trod? We think there is. And it is hoped that every one who gives this little book a perusal will, before closing it, think so too.

In small, neat handwriting, and with her accustomed felicity of expression, MRS. SHAW has penned a Sketch of her early life.

Above a hundred years ago, on the 19th of April, 1773,—before John Wesley's evangelistic tours were ended, or Charles Wesley's muse was silenced, or John Fletcher's " Checks " were completed, or Dr. Coke had declared himself a Methodist ; before the thirtieth Conference had met, or a stone of City Road Chapel had been laid; before the battle of Bunker's Hill had been fought, or Wellington or Bonaparte had attained his fourth year— Elizabeth Flamank was born. Her native place was St. Austell, in Cornwall ; " a neat little town, on the side of a fruitful hill." Mr. Wesley often visited it; and whenever he, or any of his " helpers," were in that neighbourhood, they found a hearty welcome in her father's house.

" My parents," Mrs. Shaw writes, " were members of the Methodist Society, and also regular attendants at the Established Church. It was their endeavour to instil religious principles into my mind from infancy; and their attempts were not fruitless, for when very young, before I was five years old, I remember to have felt a wish to die, and go to heaven with my mother, if God should take her hence. I delighted much in the company and conversation of pious persons, and was pleased when my mother would allow me to accompany her to her band-meeting, which was held in an upper room in our house."

When between nine and ten years of age, it was Elizabeth's honour—for such she considered it—to travel with Mr. Wesley in his chaise, while he visited some of the Societies in West Cornwall. Long, long afterwards, when old age had come, she was pleased to entertain visitors by referring to this journey, and relating how the venerable minister and the little girl had played " bo-peep " as they rode on together. She was thought too young to attend the service

at Gwennap Pit when Mr. Wesley preached
to the thousands who flocked to hear. "He
left the next morning," Mrs. Shaw writes,
" and proceeded to Mr. Wood's, at Port
Isaac, taking me with him in his carriage."

In 1783 Elizabeth was sent to a school at
Penzance. Here an incident occurred which
—though some might regard it as trivial—
made a deep impression on her mind and
was looked back upon in after-years with
much regret. To screen a school-fellow,
who had acted dishonestly, she told an
untruth. Happy for her that conscience
at once troubled her and gave her to see the
greatness of the sin she had committed!
"Alas!" she says, " how was I robbed of my
peace! and what sad depravity did I discover! Surely parents and teachers should
be careful, unless well assured of their
possessing good principles, never to suffer
the innocent, unwary and inexperienced to
mingle with those whose education has been
loose and unheeded!"

In her diary she gratefully mentions three
escapes from drowning while yet a girl:—
on one occasion at Penzance, when search-

ing among the rocks for different kinds of
sea-weed; again when crossing the Hayle
sands; and yet again when riding through
the water at high tide, near Par, a small
seaport about four miles from St. Austell.

After a brief residence at Penzance, Elizabeth returned home. "In the year 1784,"
she writes, "the Conference appointed
Messrs. F. Wrigley, W. Church, and A.
Clarke to travel in the East Cornwall
Circuit, and such a revival took place in
St. Austell at that time as has not been
equalled since. Though very young, I was
deeply affected, and as I saw many around
me brought from darkness to light and
enabled to rejoice in a sin-pardoning God, I
longed to experience the same blessing. I
wished to be happy; and, though I had no
clear perception of the plan of salvation, I
sought the Lord in prayer, and delighted in
the means of grace; and on Monday, the
3rd of January, 1785, I received a note of
admission into the Methodist Society from
Mr. Adam Clarke."

This small, time-tarnished scrap of paper
was put into my hand by its owner—who,

it need not be said, highly valued it—not
long before her decease.   It has written on
it these words :—

> " St. Austle Society.
> Admitted on tryal,
> Eliza. Flamank, Jan. 3, 1785.
> Adam Clarke."

The young evangelist by whom this note
was given found in the East Cornwall
Circuit—extending over a large tract of
country, and comprehending more than
forty preaching-places—much to hearten on
the one hand, much to dishearten on the
other.   He had to spend a great part of
his time in the saddle, the roads were not
of the best, and " the accommodations
were in most places very indifferent."   But
what more than compensated for these dis-
comforts was the success with which God
favoured him and his colleagues.   He saw
crowded congregations, a great eagerness to
hear the Word, and a revival in almost every
part of the Circuit.

" In St. Austell the heavenly flame
broke out in an extraordinary manner,

and great numbers were gathered into the
fold of Christ, among whom was Mr.
Samuel Drew, a young man then termina-
ting his apprenticeship to a shoemaker, and
afterwards distinguished as one of the first
metaphysicians of the age." In a letter to
a friend at Trowbridge, Mr. Clarke wrote :—
" Among the children there is a most blessed
movement. Numbers of them, being made
sensible of their need of Christ, have set
their feet in the paths of the Lord, and are
running with steady pace to their heavenly
Father's kingdom; and are, contrary to the
nature of things, turned fathers to the aged.
At St. Austell the Lord has lately laid to
His hand, and there is such a revival now
in it as I have never seen in any place
before. Our chapel, though the largest in
the Circuit, is so filled that the people are
obliged to stand on the seats to make room.
Last Sunday night I preached there, and
was forced to enter at the window to get to
the pulpit."

It is no wonder that in the midst of these
blessed scenes and influences Elizabeth was
led to seek the Lord, and desire union with

His people. Of the many gathered into the
Church during that time of gracious visitation, every one has ere this fallen asleep.

Notwithstanding the scoffs and sneers of
former companions, encouraged by a loving,
pious step-mother, the youthful disciple held
on her way, and continued to meet in Class,
under the leadership of a good old Methodist, Mr. Thomas Halls, father-in-law of Mr.
Samuel Drew, until February, 1786, when
she left home for Miss Bishop's school at
Keynsham, near Bristol. " Here," she
writes, " the strictest discipline was en-
forced, the school was well regulated, and
great order was preserved. Our morals
were guarded, and religious instruction was
frequently given, both by Miss Bishop, who
carefully watched over us, and by the
preachers, who came regularly according to
plan. The affectionate admonitions and
exhortations of that eminently pious man,
Mr. J. Valton, made deep impressions on
the minds of most of the young ladies, and
on mine in particular. It was during my
stay at Keynsham that I had the honour
and privilege of hearing Mrs. Fletcher give

an exhortation in the chapel to the young
people. When on a visit to Bristol, Mr.
Wesley being in the city, my father sent me
to knock at the door of his room over the
old chapel in Broadmead.* He opened it
and exclaimed, ' What ! my little Betsey !
how came you here?' This is one proof of
his extraordinary memory in recollecting
persons and names. I was then a hundred
and fifty miles from home, and had not
seen him for perhaps a year and a half."

At the Conference held in Bristol in
1786 " little Betsey " was led by Mr.
Wesley into the Conference Chapel, that
she might see the preachers assembled
there; and, if her memory were not at fault,
it was during the same visit to the city that
she dined with John and Charles Wesley at
Mr. Crosse's, in Wine Street, occupying a
seat next to Charles.

At Miss Bishop's school Elizabeth made
satisfactory progress in her studies; and her
general deportment was all that could be
desired. Her school-fellows confided in her

---

* Now used as a place of worship by the Welsh
Calvinistic Methodists.

word, paid deference to her judgment, and
treated her with kindness and respect; while
by her diligence and attention to duty she
won the approbation of her teachers.

In a letter to her granddaughter, Miss
Solomon, now the wife of the Rev. James
W. Eacott, she makes pleasing reference to
her school days :—" When I was about your
age at school," wrote Mrs. Shaw in 1852,
" my lessons were numerous, and sometimes
difficult, particularly my French lessons. I
felt conscious that all was known to my
Heavenly Father, and that He could help
me to understand and get through them.
To Him I made known my daily request,
and often have I been astonished at my
success, and grateful for the aid vouchsafed.
I do not remember ever to have been
punished or reproved as my fellow pupils
sometimes were.   Pray much, sincerely,
importunately ; and use all diligence, remembering that faith and works must be
united.   That beautiful passage often
occurs to my mind, ' Let the word of
Christ dwell in you richly in all wisdom,'
Colossians iii. 16; and also good old Mr.

Entwisle's favourite motto, (Proverbs iii. 6,) 'In all thy ways acknowledge Him, and He shall direct thy paths.'"

On Elizabeth's return home her besetment, she tells us, was love of dress. Not that she wore anything gay, "such as bows of ribbon on her bonnet:" her father would not allow that; and, moreover, eighty years ago the extravagant fashions of the present day would not have been considered in good taste. But she made it her study to get clothes of the finest and best materials, and to look "genteel" in a plain dress. This temptation proved a snare to her until, as the result of the affectionate counsels of a pious friend, Miss M. Paynter, of Redruth, and the ministry of Dr. Coke, she determined to "lay aside" the besetting sin, and to serve the Lord more faithfully and zealously than she had previously done. While, however, the fear of God was before her eyes, the love of God was not as yet shed abroad in her heart: she was still

> "A stranger to the Gospel hope,
> The sense of sin forgiven;"

and not until the 19th of May, 1793, did

she obtain a clear sense of her acceptance with God.

The narrative, as given by herself, is this:—" The Rev. Francis Truscott called at my father's, and dined with us. Having an opportunity of speaking to him alone, I told him freely the state of my mind. He kindly encouraged me to hope, and to believe that God would accept the sacrifice that Jesus Christ had made of Himself for me; adding, 'Now, even this moment, if you will but cast your soul on the mercy of God through Christ, I am sure you will obtain a sense of His pardoning love. Yes, my soul for thine, but He will bless thee.' And, glory be ascribed to my kind, long-suffering God ! I was enabled to lay hold on the Saviour, and to feel pardon and acceptance through Him."

Elizabeth could now " rejoice in the Lord;" and so great was her love to Him that she gladly denied herself of part of the time usually devoted to sleep, that she might read, and meditate, and pray. Law's " Serious Call to a Devout and Holy Life," a book much admired by Dr. Johnson, and from which the Wesleys derived benefit, became her companion; and the character of Miranda appeared to her so attractive that there was danger of her becoming ascetical in her views and practices. Happily, God's blessing on the conversation of pious friends prevented this evil.

CHAPTER II.

THE CHRISTIAN MAIDEN.

In the possession of new-found joy and peace, it was Elizabeth's immediate desire and resolve to do something for her Lord. Saved herself, she sought the salvation of others. She did not hesitate to speak to friends and neighbours about the things which belonged to their peace. She read the Scriptures to the poor in their own homes; and, in other ways, as opportunities were presented to her, she strove to be useful.

When the Rev. Joseph Benson visited Cornwall, in 1795, and with such power and success preached the Word to the tens of thousands who were eager to hear him, Elizabeth could not remain at home. How many times she heard the celebrated preacher I cannot say, but the services of the memorable twenty-first of June were never forgotten by her. When on that midsummer Sabbath afternoon Mr. Benson addressed the crowd before the market-house at Redruth, on "Thou art weighed in the balances, and art found wanting," (Daniel v. 27,) she was there. And again in the evening, when he preached at Gwennap Pit to about twenty thousand persons, on the Last Judgment, taking as his text, " I saw the dead, small and great, stand before God, etc.," (Rev. xx. 12,) she was there ; and the impression made by these services was not effaced, even when fourscore years and more had passed away.

A letter, written to a relative before the year closed, sets forth the state of her mind, as well as the avidity with which she seized every opportunity of working for God at this early period of her Christian life. The following extracts, though somewhat lengthy, are too excellent to be omitted.

"St. Austell,

"24th December, 1795.

"MY DEAR AUNT,—

"I have many times thought of writing you, but hitherto one thing or another has prevented. . . . . . Though 'absent in body,' I cannot help feeling for you in your distress. However, this is certain, that 'every gift of God is good,' not even afflictions and sufferings excepted. For though it be oftentimes the case that the dispensations of Divine Providence appear to us, poor, blind mortals, dark and mysterious, yet the Word of God cannot fail: 'All things work together for good to them that love God.' The cup is mixed by His unerring Hand Who deals tenderly with His children, and 'will not suffer them to be tempted above that they are able,' and will certainly 'with the temptation also make a way to escape.' A beautiful remark of a pious man was this: 'The greatest blessing which the Almighty can bestow on us is affliction, and grace to bear it.' I believe it is the means of drawing us more closely to our merciful High Priest, and of giving us to feel that without His support we can do nothing.

"It is good to be taught wisdom and humble love while sitting at the foot of the Cross. There we may find the sweetest

food. I have often thought lately that the
Lord has begun to ' purge His floor '—to
separate the chaff from the wheat. O that
we may not faint in the day of trial, knowing that ' he that endureth to the end shall
be saved'! May He ride on till all are
subdued, till He gains a glorious Church,
without spot, and unblamable before Him
in love. . . . . . Can we not say that He is
indeed the only Fountain of all good, of life,
love, peace and truth, a never-failing Friend?
Why then should we shrink from suffering ;
from that which has a tendency to conform
us unto Him ' in the likeness of His death'?
O that we may be partakers of ' His resurrection '! May the Lord enable you to
mount above the storms, and make you to
' sit in heavenly places in Christ Jesus '!
Set no dependence on man. Trust not in
an arm of flesh, which is liable to error and
change ; but ' trust in the Lord for ever,' for
in Him is ' everlasting strength.' Whatever
you lose, you may find more than all in Him.
Suffer not men nor devils to hinder you
from ' pressing toward the mark for the
prize of the high calling of God in Christ

Jesus.' Remember God is the same. Endeavour to look beyond this vale of sorrows to the heavenly Canaan where all tears are wiped away; for the promise is that ' to them who by patient continuance in well doing seek for glory and honour and immortality, eternal life ' shall be the reward. For my own part, I want to feel more of the quickening influences of Divine love, to die daily to self and sin, and to be more diligent in wisdom's ways. I have great reason to be thankful both for past and present mercies : above all for Jesus Christ, and the least hope of being admitted at the last to be with Him, and to see Him as He is. That each of us may so run as to obtain is the sincere desire of

"Your affectionate Niece,

"E. Flamank."

The nineteenth century has undoubtedly been a period of unparalleled development and progress. What marvellous changes— social, commercial, political, religious— have been brought about since the foregoing letter was written! To mention nothing else, the application of steam to purposes of locomotion now enables travellers to get over as much ground in a day as would have required at least a week when the century began.

Notes of a journey taken in 1796 indicate a marked contrast to the present rapid, comfortable, and comparatively safe mode of travelling. No gas in the towns, no telegraph wires by the roadside, no liveried postmen with their heavy burdens of correspondence and parcels, no large factories, no railways, no puffing, hurrying fire-horse, were then to be seen. She writes :—

" *July* 19*th.*—Set off with my sister for Trowbridge.

" *July* 21*st.*—Reached Bristol.

" *July* 25*th.*—Bath.   Heard Mr. Collins at King Street.

" *July* 26*th.*—Went to Trowbridge.   Met in Mrs. Pond's Class.

" *July* 28*th.*—Bradford.

" *July* 29*th.*—Returned to Bristol.

"*August 2nd.*—Miss Ritchie and Miss Johnson's conversation excellent.* Prayer-meeting at eleven o'clock at Mrs. Pine's. In the afternoon Miss Ritchie read a letter from Lady Maxwell, expressive of deep self-abasement and close fellowship with God. Such lettings into Deity! Such views of heaven!

"*August 4th.*—Breakfasted with Miss Ritchie at Miss Johnson's. A treat indeed!

"*August 5th.*—Left Bristol for Wellington. When within a mile of this place the coach overturned. All, except myself, hurt or much frightened. My mind calm and peaceful. Thankful for preserving mercy.

"*August 8th.*—Exeter.

"*August 9th.*—Plymouth.

"*August 11th.*—Home."

---

* "Betsy Ritchie, Miss Johnson, and M. Clarke are women after my own heart."
John Wesley to Adam Clarke.

"I am persuaded you will yourself profit as much, if not more, by the conversation of a few in Bristol, Mr. Valton and Miss Johnson in particular, as by that of any persons in Great Britain."
John Wesley to R. C. Brackenbury.

What cause for joy would it be if all our Methodist young people of the present day were as eager to attend the means of grace, social as well as public, as the above entry shows Elizabeth to have been!

In looking over her diary I find the difficulty to be that of selection. The extracts must of necessity be few, and where there is so much of an interesting nature it is not easy to decide what those few shall be. The following, written prior to her marriage, will be read with pleasure:—

" *October 2nd*, 1796.—I desire to praise the Lord from my soul for the past week. ' He giveth power to the faint; and to them that have no might He increaseth strength.' Last Monday I felt my soul quickened, and a heavy burden removed from my mind. The Lord doeth all things well.

" *Tuesday.*—Went to Polmear to hear preaching. Found it good to be there; and felt much love to the precious souls who likewise came to hear.

" *Wednesday.* — Spent some time in profitable conversation with my dear father, and in the evening found great liberty in

recommending the service of my blessed
Master to a lady of Bristol, whom I had
never seen before. If it should prove useful
to her, to God be all the glory!

"*Friday and yesterday.*—Dropped a few
words to some poor sinners who yet remain
in ignorance respecting their souls' salvation
amid 'this blaze of Gospel day.' Lord,
teach them to escape for their lives to Thee
ere it prove too late!

"*May* 21*st*, 1797.—I awoke this morning
with these words :—

> 'My soul, and all its powers,
>   Thine, wholly Thine, shall be ;
> All, all my happy hours
>   I consecrate to Thee.'

Amen, Lord Jesus! Strengthen me to
perform the covenant; forgive my wanderings from Thee, and keep me near Thy
side.

"*September* 27*th.*—This morning I felt
strong desires for the recovery of a backslider, and had liberty in praying for her.
In the forenoon I was called into the shop
to settle an account with her; and I gladly
embraced the opportunity of speaking to

her of the danger of living without God.
She then told me that she felt the Spirit
striving with her, and that she had been
particularly affected under a sermon which
she had lately heard.

" *October 3rd.*—Quarterly Meeting. A
blessed day. The power and presence of
the Highest overshadowed the preachers
and leaders in the afternoon ; and in the
evening at the Lovefeast we were not less
favoured. God spoke peace to two troubled
hearts, and many present had cause to
rejoice in His salvation. After some time
the house was filled with strong crying, etc. ;
some praying, others singing, and others
speaking of the goodness of God to their
souls. The noise rather discomposed my
mind; for though I durst not condemn, yet
I find the most profitable seasons are when
there is a silent breathing after God, and a
' sacred awe which dares not move.' Lord
Jesus, shed Thy love abroad in every heart !

" *October 12th.*—This afternoon visited
several poor families, and found a present
reward. In one house felt it good to hear a
poor old Zionward traveller, (who had tasted

of the good word of God, and walked in the narrow path, through storms and difficulties, upwards of forty years,) tell of the goodness of God to her soul. She wept, and could not express what she then experienced of His mercy and love. . . . . . She entertained the preachers at her own house for twenty-seven years, and is thankful for the many opportunities she had of their advice, instruction, and prayers. She is now near eighty-two, just arrived at the desired haven, with a goodly prospect of the better country, and no doubt of landing safe.

" *October* 17*th*.—Mr. B. and I called to see John and Nanny Bray, at Penforder, two old travellers, who are got almost to their journey's end, and have a blessed prospect in view. I went up stairs to see the bed which the preachers sleep in, and found it, as I had been told, decorated with ever-green curtains. The ivy had crept through the wall or window, and was curiously en-twined about the bed.

" *November* 14*th*.—Visited many objects of distress. Several in the workhouse confined to their beds, breathing out their wretched existence without hope of a better, either in this world or in that which is to come. In one room found a blind man sitting by his poor afflicted wife, who is a cripple, confined to her bed, in a deplorable condition. Even those who are in tolerable health, and feel any concern for their immortal souls, are surrounded by others whose oaths and curses render their situation extremely uncomfortable. I felt great liberty in speaking to those whom I saw there. From thence I went to see a poor woman, who after her confinement had caught cold. Here was a scene of deep poverty. She had not a bit of straw to lie on ; and, being on the ground-floor, the room was damp. She had formerly felt desires to serve God, but never heartily sought Him ; and now she feels anguish of spirit from a sense of His displeasure and her ingratitude. O what trouble do some undergo ! Lord, give me a thankful and obedient heart for all Thy multiplied blessings continually bestowed upon me, and teach me to be a faithful and wise steward.

" *December* 12*th.*—Mr. Hore, of Dock,

purser of the 'Venerable,' who was on
board during the late engagement, gave us
a particular account of the action; * and said
he never saw the interposition of Providence
so wonderfully displayed in his life before.
Had they lost only ten minutes in the beginning they would have done nothing. . . .
According to my views of Christianity, war
and bloodshed, with all their dire train of
calamities, are as contrary to the spirit of
the Gospel of Jesus Christ as light is
opposed to darkness. It is truly painful that
so many thousands should be hurried into
eternity, the greater part of whom, I believe
I may justly fear, are unprepared to meet
the Judge. O ye princes and rulers of the
people, what account will ye be able to give
in the last great day?

"*December* 21*st.*—Mr. Hodgson preached
last night from Job xxiii. 3—6, and towards
the end of the sermon a man stood up and
said: 'Glory be to God; I know it, I feel
it; I feel the truth of it now in my heart!'

---

* Admiral Duncan defeated the Dutch fleet off
Camperdown, on the Coast of Holland, October 11th,
1797.

This encourages us to hope for a greater revival of vital religion. I look forward to next Tuesday (the day of the Quarterly Meeting) with pleasing expectation of an outpouring of the Spirit on the people, who are, I hear, alive to God. Who can tell the 'wondrous power of faithful prayer,' when many are agreed in their petitions to the God of all grace? Last night, as I was sitting at work, I felt such a sense of the love of God to my soul as I seldom experience: my heart melted as wax before the fire, and truly God was all in all.

" *December* 27th. — Yesterday was our Quarterly Meeting, and a most remarkable time we had. At the Lovefeast, I felt my mind stayed upon God, and my prayer was that He would manifest Himself as a mighty Saviour. After a few persons had spoken, Mr. B. desired the gardener Stephens to pray, and before he concluded many cried aloud for mercy. When the noise began I felt my spirit agitated, and my heart hardened, but soon I was enabled to look to Jesus, and, glory be to Him! I found Him strong to deliver. From that time nothing outward

disturbed me. It seemed as though I was
surrounded with God. One young woman
who sat near me groaned, being burthened.
I desired one of the preachers to come and
pray with her. He did so, and several others
joined in supplication in her behalf. I
desired her to look to Jesus as a present
Saviour, to cast her soul on His atoning
blood, etc. I believe I did not rise from my
knees for more than two hours. My soul
travailed in birth with her till Christ was
formed in her heart. I saw so much of the
willingness of God to save, that I thought
I could almost believe for her. . . . . During
this meeting six persons obtained a sense
of pardoning love. Some were praying,
some singing, and others praising God. To
many this might have the appearance of
disorder and confusion; but, for my own
part, I was never in such a meeting before.
My soul centred in God. To-day I have
felt much of the Divine presence, and free
access to the throne of grace. I hardly
remember that I ever felt such melting,
softening, sweet dependence on Jesus before.

" *March 7th.*—This morning (Wednesday) I rode to Sticker, and heard Mr. Hodgson preach at half-past nine. At the Society-meeting tickets were given, and fourteen persons received ' Notes of Admittance.' 'Tis true they were some of ' the poor of this world;' but I trust they will strive to be ' rich in faith, and heirs of the kingdom ' of glory. I do not know that I ever felt so much love to the poor before. I could embrace them as my fellow travellers in the kingdom and patience of Jesus. When returning I observed two men before me, but fearing lest they were drunk I did not attempt to overtake them, till these words on a sudden occurred to my mind: ' Go near and join thyself' to them. I hastened on, and felt great liberty in speaking to them of the things concerning the kingdom of God. One of them had never heard a Methodist preacher till he came here to work, the other had often heard, and had many pious relatives. I invited them to 'go to the chapel at night, and was pleased to see them there."

Thus the young disciple laboured for the

Master whom she loved. Her heart was full of Christ, and hence to recommend Him to others was her great delight.

"The gardener Stephens," mentioned in a previous page, was a man of simple manners and earnest piety; mighty in prayer, and instrumental in winning many souls. His addresses were original, quaint, powerful, and withal, sometimes amusing. Hence, in referring to a watch-night service held in January, 1798, Miss Flamank writes:— "While the gardener was speaking I was so diverted at some expressions that I could not forbear laughing; and ever since, when I have thought of them, they have had the same effect." While, however, there was humour, there was also an ever manifest desire to exalt Christ and to do good; and so highly was he esteemed that there was no part of the Circuit to which he was not heartily welcomed. The well-known story of the Leek-seed Chapel has won him fame of which he never dreamt. Near the entrance to that chapel I have often looked on the tombstone which marks the spot where the old man's body sleeps. Time, though doing its work, has not yet rendered illegible the inscription which tells the passer-by who cares to read that " William Stephens almost suddenly exchanged the toils of earth for the rest of heaven, on Saturday, December 7th, 1822, aged eighty years."

CHAPTER III.

THE MINISTER'S WIFE.

FROM a worldly point of view some of the offers of marriage made to Miss Flamank were all that could be desired. She might have had position and wealth, but these did not satisfy her ambition; for she had learnt that "he builds too low who builds beneath the skies." And, moreover, she was determined never to give her hand without her heart. Her father, with mistaken affection, felt great disappointment, and manifested not a little displeasure at the course she considered it her duty to pursue. But she had counted the cost, and her resolve was to be thoroughly devoted to God and wholly engaged in His service.

After much prayerful consideration she became engaged to the Rev. Robert Green, a worthy young minister who was stationed in the St. Austell Circuit in 1797; and on the twenty-fifth anniversary of her birthday they were married. This was a step which, though it did not meet with the hearty approval of some of her relatives, she never saw occasion to regret. To her husband she gave a true wifely love; and, during the little time they were permitted to live together, they were helpers of each other's joy.

In what spirit and with what zeal she set about her duties as a minister's wife may be seen by the following extracts from her diary:—

"*April* 6*th*, 1798.—I need much of the grace of the Holy Spirit to instruct and guide me that I may be useful to others, and faithful to my own soul. Without love I am nothing.

"Fowey, *April* 22*nd.*—On Thursday last, after breakfast, in retirement I found it good to draw near to God. We then went to the Church and entered into the solemn engagement to take each other for life. My mind was composed, and I trust we each entered into covenant with God to serve Him and promote His glory. This morning I felt it to be a precious season at the

D

prayer-meeting. After our return some
friends joined us, and their souls seemed
truly engaged with God in our behalf. O
blessed Saviour, teach me to do Thy will,
and 'lead me in the way everlasting'!

" Poole, *April 29th.*—'What hath God
wrought!' O that all my powers may unite
to adore His Almighty wisdom and goodness!
. . . . . . He has highly favoured me with
the blessings of His providence and grace,
and still He invites me to partake of His
bounty. O for a keener appetite for the
Bread of Life! Last Tuesday we bade
farewell to Cornwall, and were mercifully
preserved on the journey; but had a narrow
escape from being overturned in a muddy
river. Slept at Mr. Lessey's, Dock, where
we were hospitably entertained. On Wednesday we arrived at Exeter, between four
and five o'clock, and on the following
morning at three we took the coach for
Blandford. I embraced an opportunity of
speaking to several fellow passengers. May
it not be in vain! The coach was very near
being overturned when going down Char-
mouth Hill, but here also our kind Pre-

server watched over us, and kept us from harm. From Blandford we came on to Poole in a post chaise. Blessed Lord! crown us with mercies and loving-kindness for Thy great Name's sake.

"*May* 20*th.*—Last Sunday night my dear Robert preached to a large congregation with much zeal and liberty. I believe many felt the word and trembled. I was much concerned for their eternal happiness, and thought I could even lay down my own life to save a soul from sin and the devil. On Wednesday night, at the prayer-meeting, I attempted to supplicate the throne of grace, but was uncommonly exercised. I felt no access to God. My mind was confused. I was really grieved, both on my own account and on account of others. When leaving I was ashamed to look up, or speak to any one. Friends sympathize.l and tried to encourage me, but their words seemed as idle tales."

After such a humiliation as that of which mention is here made, many would have determined never to attempt to pray in public again; but that was not Mrs. Green's

spirit. Failure once or twice, or even
thrice, was with her no reason why there
should not be perseverance. When assured
that her course was a right one, she was
prepared to press onward in it, whatever
difficulties bestrewed the way.

"Portland, *July* 8*th.* — Yesterday my
mind was much exercised in reference to
meeting the Class. I knew not what to
do. The importance of the charge rested
with great weight on me. I felt my own
weakness and insufficiency, and was not so
fully satisfied that it was my duty before
the Lord as I wished to be. Yet to stay at
home and shun the cross did not appear
right. After some deliberating I went in
fear and trembling, beseeching the Lord to
give me simplicity, and to direct my words
to the profit of the people. He graciously
vouchsafed to answer the feeble request of
His servant; and His presence was felt in
our little assembly.

"*July* 15*th.*—I see the need I have to
be circumspect in all my deportment,—in
little things as well as great, — lest I
should be only as one of those foolish

virgins who had a lamp, but no oil to keep the light burning. As I am now called to labour a little in the vineyard of my Lord, may I be found a diligent, faithful servant.

"*August 5th.*—On Wednesday, in company with Miss Holland, I visited some families and prayed with them. On Thursday, had a favourable opportunity of conversing with Dr. T., which I hope will not soon be forgotten. Afterwards spent a little time in prayer with Mrs. Atwool and some other friends. Mrs. Brackenbury, being unwell, declined going to meet the Class, so that I was obliged to go. O for greater cheerfulness to fulfil the Lord's work! When shall I be willing to deny myself in this respect?"

In a conversation with Mrs. Shaw a short time prior to her decease, and before any thought of writing this Memorial had occurred to me, I learnt that while on a visit to Portland she was persuaded by Mrs. Robert Carr Brackenbury to conduct a Class-meeting. "Only this once" had been her thought when first asked to lead; and when called on to do so again after Mrs. Brackenbury's arrival she declined. But (and there was a pleasant smile on the countenance of the aged pilgrim as she told the story) Mrs. Brackenbury insisted: " As you have sung ' A,' you must sing ' B ; ' and not think for a moment of giving up the work you have begun." From that time for above seventy years, almost without intermission, she held the honourable position of Class-leader. A touching letter, addressed to Mrs. Brackenbury forty years after the incident just mentioned took place, soliciting help for a minister's widow, in low circumstances and in feeble health,—" one of the modest, retiring few who prefer to suffer in silence rather than complain,"— contains reference to Portland and their meeting there. The following is an extract :—

" St. Austell,
" May 3rd, 1838.

" VERY DEAR MADAM,—

" So many years have elapsed since I was favoured with a personal interview that were it not for the information received by you from our highly esteemed friend Mr.

Riggall, who has occasionally visited us, you would probably have forgotten me; though while memory lasts it is not probable I should cease to think of you, and the time that I spent in Portland during your visit there in 1798. It was then that, by your persuasions, and I may add command, I tremblingly attempted to meet a Class. Since that time in this means of grace my soul has been often watered from on high. . . . May I be found faithful ! "

After the Conference of 1798 Mr. Green removed to Southampton, where he and his dear wife gave themselves heartily and hopefully to their hallowed work.

" Southampton, *August* 19*th*, 1798.—On Tuesday we arrived here in safety. At one of the halting places I took the opportunity of speaking freely to a young woman. She seemed to listen attentively, but soon after went out to the rest of the company, who had before quitted the room one by one when the subject of religion was introduced. How many are wilfully ignorant of the things which belong unto their peace !

Just after we left the carriage some men, standing in the street, said, without our asking, 'Mr. Clarke lives at the corner house in the square.' So true is it that man looketh at, and judgeth by the outward appearance, even the shallow mark of plain dress. Our kind friends seemed glad to receive us. I trust we shall be united in one spirit to promote the Redeemer's kingdom in this place, and have cause to rejoice in our labour.

" *October 7th.*—This afternoon I have had some profitable reflections on the providence and power of God while reading 1 Kings xviii., xix. With Obadiah I can say, 'I fear the Lord from my youth.'

" *November 4th.*—On Monday and Tuesday visited most of the members of our Society, and felt satisfaction in being so employed.

" *December 23rd.* — Blessed be God for His continued mercies towards me, an unworthy, unprofitable servant! What shall I render unto my bountiful Benefactor? He requires me to love Him with all my heart, mind, soul, and strength; but O, how short do I daily come! Lord, draw and bind me to Thyself, that I may not wander from Thee. . . . Last Wednesday our new chapel was opened by Messrs. Smith, Algar, and Byron. I felt an awful solemnity resting on my mind, and gratitude to the Lord for providing a house where His Name might be exalted.

" *January 20th,* 1799.—I feel it good to call to remembrance the past dealings of the Lord with my soul. He is indeed abundant in goodness and truth. On hearing part of the account of Mrs. Fletcher's death read last evening, my desires were increased for entire devotedness to God, and conformity to His lovely likeness.

" *February 10th.*—I feel my soul taking refuge in the wounds of my crucified Lord; and I trust I shall never rest but in His all-atoning sacrifice. Dr. Coke has paid us a visit, and given us pleasing accounts respecting the release of our friends in the Island of Jersey, and the kind interference of Government in their behalf.* O that this

---

* In Jersey a municipal law required that the militia should turn out for drilling on the Sabbath, and power was sought to enforce the penalty of banishment on those

instance of our Heavenly Father's love may be gratefully acknowledged by all His children !

"*March 3rd.*—This day three years ago my dear mother entered into rest, into the joy of her Lord, Whom she loved and faithfully served. O that all her children may follow her, and be made fellow heirs of immortality !

"*March 6th.* — Went to Winchester Assizes. My dear husband and I visited the Cathedral; and from thence we went to the Hall, where Judge Grose gave an excellent charge to the Grand Jury, which I thought preferable to the sermon at the Cathedral.

"*March 17th.* — In every respect I am

---

who refused to obey. Dr. Coke implored the Government to withhold the required sanction, and notwithstanding great opposition persevered in his efforts until they were crowned with complete success. "I have been endeavouring," he wrote, "to put an end to a persecution of our people which was carried on for about six years. The Lord has given me the hearts of the king and his council, and enabled me to bring the business to a happy conclusion."—*Vide* Etheridge's "Life of the Rev. Thomas Coke, D.C.L."

favourably situated for making swift
progress in the Divine life ; and therefore I
am left without excuse ; but I feel the in-
dolence of my nature and a backward,
unbelieving heart, to be my secret, subtle
enemies. In how many shapes will sloth
appear ! I must cry out with David, ' My
soul cleaveth unto the dust : quicken Thou
me according to Thy word.'

" *March* 24*th.*—Easter Day. Glory be to
God ! His mercy, power, and love are still
manifested toward me, notwithstanding my
ingratitude toward Him. How many deliverances has He wrought out for me during
the past twelve months ! His hand has
supplied all my wants, and ' the lines are
fallen unto me in pleasant places.' I have
felt my soul raised in gratitude to Him this
day for His infinite love to fallen man.

" *April* 19*th.*—Much comforted with the
glorious news from Cornwall of the revival
of the Work of God. O that the flames may
spread over the whole earth !

" *May* 5*th.*—In visiting many of our friends
this week I have been blessed. The Lord
has given me utterance in my approaches to

Him, and we hear of many returning to the Lord, both backsliders and others. Glory be to His holy Name !

" *July 7th.*—I see it to be my duty and privilege to live in the spirit of sacrifice, yielding up myself unreservedly to the living God. I am grieved when I hear of professors walking disorderly, and wish to feel more on their account, as well as to experience more sympathy for those who are tried, persecuted, and afflicted. O that the spirit of conviction may seize upon the thousands who are now assembled at the camp, and cause them to ' flee from the wrath to come,' and seek redemption through the merits of a crucified Saviour !

" *July 21st.*—I have felt utterance and liberty in speaking to sinners of the things that belong unto their peace. On Wednesday afternoon walked up to the camp (a scene of distress and dissipation indeed), and had an opportunity of conversing with some who fear the Lord. In returning home, Sergeant A. and another whom we had been in search of, while going to an ale-house in search of some of the disorderly characters, overtook us. I felt a pity and love for these two backsliders, which constrained me to speak as tenderly, closely, affectionately, and earnestly as I think I ever did to any. I trust God blessed the word.

"*July* 28*th.*—Since Thursday my mind has been exercised from seeing my dear husband so ill. This dispensation has appeared rather mysterious. Still the Lord has graciously supported me, and I have been enabled to trust in Him. Though I do not see for what end at present, yet by-and-by I doubt not the secret will be revealed, and I shall praise Him. I desire to feel more sensibly my obligations to the Lord for His mercies, and hope I shall be preserved from a murmuring spirit, under every affliction."

As Mr. Green's illness continued, and it was thought that change of air and horse exercise might be beneficial to him, at the close of the year he was appointed to New-bury. In Southampton he and his wife had met with much to cheer. The kindness of the people and the success which God had given endeared the place to them; and not without mutual regrets were farewells spoken, and the journey to the new Circuit begun.   Mrs. Green writes, " The union we felt with our kind, dear friends there made it painful to part from them.   Never did I expect to suffer so much from parting with any people as I did in leaving them.   The affection and esteem manifested by them demand a return.   May the Lord bless them with grace and truth ! "

The " affection and esteem " were never forgotten, as is proved by the following extracts from a letter written to George Laishley, Esq., fifty years afterwards :—

" November 15th, 1849.

" DEAR SIR,—

" In reading the *Watchman* a short time since I was delighted and thankful to find that such a noble effort is being made at Southampton to build a new chapel.   May it be the spiritual birthplace of many thousands of immortal souls !

" In the year 1798 the Portsmouth Circuit was divided, and Southampton

made the head of a new one. It was ther
that I accompanied my first husband, the
late Robert Green, thither. We had neithe
chapel nor preacher's house, although botl
were in course of building, and the forme
was opened on the 19th of December follow
ing. Before that our place of worship wa
an upper room in a street leading dow1
from East Street towards the Canal, by th
side of which the chapel and preacher'
house were built.

"My dear husband's illness was the caus
of our removal to a Circuit where he coul
have the benefit of horse exercise. Whil
memory lasts never shall I forget th
extreme kindness and sympathy of our dea
friends at Southampton while we were witl
them, and afterwards during our short sta
at Newbury, and when we removed to Bath
So many years have passed away tha
probably very few, if any, of those wh
knew me now remain. Should there be any
I desire to present my love and gratefu
remembrances of their kindness.

"As I wish to have a stone in the build
ing, I beg your acceptance of the enclose

trifle. Let it be put down as from 'A Cornish Friend.'

"Sincerely praying that all your works may be begun, continued, and ended with a single eye to the glory of God, and that His especial blessing may ever attend and rest upon you, and all the true-hearted friends of Wesleyan-Methodism,

"I remain, dear Sir,

"Yours very respectfully,

"ELIZABETH SHAW."

The hoped-for improvement in the state of Mr. Green's health was not realised. His illness not only continued, but increased, and before many weeks had passed another removal was found necessary. With an afflicted husband and a helpless babe, born very soon after their arrival at Newbury, there was much in Mrs. Green's circumstances calculated to depress; but she knew that though the cup was bitter, the hand of Love had mixed it. Her confidence in God remained unshaken, and, in the spirit of true piety, she bowed to the Father's will. On October 6th, a few days before leaving Newbury for Bath, she

wrote :—" I have lately passed through deep
waters, and the floods have nearly over-
whelmed me; but blessed be my Rock and
sure Foundation! He has made bare His
holy arm, and thus far helped me. Now
let an altar be raised unto Jehovah, and
let ' all that is within me, praise His holy
Name.' O that my trust and confidence
in Omnipotence may be more abundantly
strengthened!"

It soon became apparent that the medi-
cinal waters of Bath were of no avail.
Nothing could arrest the progress of the
disease of which Mr. Green was the subject,
and in January, 1800, the Lord took him
to Himself. When the friend who sat up
with him during his last night said, " God
is love, my brother," he replied, " He is; I
know He is." Shortly after he said, " I
shall praise Him for ever; for ever and ever
Yes, I shall." These were his last words.

In perfect peace, without a struggle or a
sigh, he fell asleep. The widow, in the
midst of her deep sorrow, turned to her
diary, and made the following entry :—
" What to write or how to describe my

feelings I know not ; but thus far the Lord
has been with me, and supported me under
the severest trial human nature can bear.
I mourn for the great loss of the kindest,
tenderest, and most affectionate husband
that ever woman was blessed with.   In
truth I can say I never received an unkind
word or look from him ; but everything as
much the reverse as possible.   My heart
bleeds at the painful thought that he is no
more.   My all of happiness below, as it
respected outward things, was centred in
him ; and I have frequently suspected since
the Lord took him to Himself, that I was
in great danger of resting satisfied with the
good I was in possession of, without looking
for that abundant grace which the Lord
waits to bestow on the hungry, thirsty soul.
O that I may walk more closely with God in
future ! "

After an absence of two years she who
left her father's house to become a happy
bride returned to it a stricken widow. She
went out " full," and the Lord brought her
home again "empty." And yet not "empty;"
for was there not her little child to solace

her? So she thought, as her own words indicate :—"Nothing seems to court my stay but my lovely, helpless infant. Were it not for him, how gladly would I quit this tenement, should the Lord call, to unite with my dearest friend in adoring the Triune God for evermore."

Only for a little time, however, had she the care of her darling boy. She makes mention of two or three illnesses he suffered during his short life of two years and ten months; and on one occasion, when herself indisposed, she writes :—" When I think of bidding farewell to earth, I almost desire first to see the tender plant sheltered from the storms and tempests which are inseparable from humanity." God saw that the " tender plant " could not bear the blasts of earth, and in love He removed it to the shelter of His own heaven, to which shelter the father, also a " tender plant," had been taken less than three years before.

" And the mother gave, in tears and pain,
    The flower she most did love;
  She knew she should find that flower again
    In the fields of light above."

CHAPTER IV.

WIDOWHOOD.

Soon after Mrs. Green's return to St. Austell she entered into business, the duties connected with which were not so congenial to her feelings as those which had previously required her attention, and in the discharge of which she had hoped to spend her days. Still, what she put her hand to she did with all her heart; remembering the Apostolic teaching, "Not slothful in business; fervent in spirit; serving the Lord." The guiding hand of God was recognised; and for His goodness in bestowing on her temporal comforts as well as spiritual blessings she did not cease to praise Him.

I might take many lengthy extracts from her diary, written during her widowhood, all indicating zeal for God, love to His cause, and eagerness "to know and do

His perfect will." The following must
suffice :—

"*May 4th*, 1800.—I pray that I may learn
wisdom from the things which I suffer ; but
to follow a crucified Saviour is not an easy
thing. Nature shrinks; though I believe a
suffering path to be an honourable one,
because it has a tendency to beget in the
soul a likeness to its living Head.

"*June 4th.*—The more I see of pious
Quakers the more I admire them, and long
to drink in their spirit. Not that I feel
any inclination to become a member of their
Society ; for I esteem my privileges among
the Methodists greater than I could find in
any other sect: and I see now, as I have
always seen, that my duty is to abide where
I have been called and blessed.

"*June 15th.*—Strange and unexpected
things have occurred as it respects my tem-
porals. I am conscious that my motives
are such as will be approved of by God.
At the same time there appear emptiness,
meanness, and poor earthly nothingness in
my present situation in comparison with my
late choice, when I gladly forsook the

honours and riches of this world, and went out, not knowing whither, to be engaged in the best work. I trust the Lord will direct me, enable me to honour Him with what He is pleased to bestow, and keep me from worldly-mindedness.

"*July* 27*th.*—Yesterday was the day appointed for beginning to value the stock. I set about my part without anxiety. May I be preserved from the spirit of the world and taught to look to the heavenly inheritance which is reserved for the faithful !

"*August* 10*th.*—Many circumstances serve to bring my loss continually to my remembrance. On Monday night I received an account from Conference of the stations of the preachers. May they be useful—men of clean hands, and zealous for the glory of the living God !

"*September* 14*th.*—I wish to feel my soul more drawn out in contemplation on the eternal world, and to live in constant expectation of the blessed change. O for an increase of vital religion, and heartfelt union with the Source of immortal blessedness ! The Lord graciously condescends to bless me with refreshings from His presence amidst the trials to which I am exposed.

'O what is earth, if heaven be mine?'

" *September* 28*th.* — Great is the com-passion of God towards me, notwithstanding my many revoltings, my unfaithfulness, and barrenness in His vineyard. Last Sunday was a good day. I know not when I have been so much blessed. Yet I have con-stant need to pray, 'Quicken me in Thy righteousness.' On Wednesday much tried from some persons in the shop having too much liquor.* I was condemned for not resolutely denying it; and felt a determina-tion never to yield any more to importunities or threats. *Let the consequence be what it may, I am resolved that I will never buy custom at the expense of sinning against God.*

" *October* 26*th.* — My desires have been going out after God and contentment in Him. I pray to be preserved from the love

---

* When the above was written it was common in some parts of Cornwall for shopkeepers to supply their best customers with drink. Happily the custom has now become well-nigh obsolete.

of the world, and from every temper and
disposition contrary to His will.

"*November* 16*th.*—My soul has been
blessed this morning while reading the
Sermon ' On Prayer ' in the March Magazine. I see its excellency ; but want to
enjoy that heart-felt fellowship with God at
all times which will enable me to live above
the world. On Wednesday I walked down
to the workhouse, and saw many of the poor.
In praying with a man who died the next
morning I felt liberty and access to God.

"*December* 14*th.*—This past week I have
had some good seasons at family prayer.
Last night at the Class-meeting the love of
God was so powerfully manifested to me
that I could scarcely refrain from weeping
aloud. I feel—as I have not done for a long
time—that I can

'praise Him for all that is past,
And trust Him for all that's to come.'

"*January* 4*th*, 1801.—Sixteen years ago
yesterday, Mr. A. Clarke gave me a note of
admission. Glory be to God, my face is
still Zionward, and my desire is to live to
and for Him Who has bought me with His

own blood! May my future days praise Him!

"*April* 12*th.*—On Monday last I rode behind E. B. to Lower St. Columb. We expected to have met three or four thousand tinners on the road, but felt no fear. However, we saw nothing of the men, and arrived in safety. On Tuesday I rode about four miles to see the nuns at Lanherne. I felt much pity for them, and gratitude to God for His enlightening, quickening grace. Had an opportunity of speaking to Mr. C. on the happiness arising from true religion, and the unsatisfying nature of everything beside. On Friday there was a disturbance in the market because of the high price of provisions. Yesterday I heard of some alarming riots. Amidst all these outward tumults, I bless God for giving me power to cast my care on Him.

"*April* 19*th.*—This day I remember with gratitude the multiplied blessings bestowed on me during twenty-eight years. Few have been my days below, but they have been chequered with sorrow and mourning, and many Fatherly chastisements, which I

believe are proofs of *His* love Who cannot
err.   On this the anniversary of my birth
and wedding day I wish to acknowledge
them as such, and bow with meek submission under the rod.   I cannot help
dropping a tear of grief, unmixed with
murmuring, at the thought of having been
so soon left to journey alone in the wilderness.   O that while I say ' Thy will be done'
the prayer may be free from selfishness, and
every disposition contrary to pure love!

"*April* 24*th.*—This morning I have been
blessed in secretly pouring out my soul before
God.   I desire to be truly and fully devoted
to Him.   I frequently seem to myself like
a bird in a cage, shut up from activity and
that liberty which the Lord once brought
me into.   I am now imprisoned in the
cage of worldly concerns—business, and all
the anxieties attending it; but I pray,
Teach and strengthen me, O Lord, that I
may

' In Thy service here employ
   The talents Thou to me hast given,
Till I gain my Master's joy,
   And reign with Him in heaven.'

I feel I cannot do this as I once could, but I hope I shall strive to do it as I can.

" *July* 26*th.*—This morning, while reading Dr. Paley's ' Evidences of Christianity ' in the July and August numbers of the Magazine, my soul has been blessed with desires for ' inward purity and a single internal purpose of pleasing God.' I see great deficiency as to the government of my thoughts. Were these laid open to view, what incoherency, wanderings, distractions, and irregularity would be discovered! O for more of that wisdom which cometh from above! On Wednesday I had some profitable conversation with a Quaker, who dined with me, respecting the outward form and the inward power of the Spirit. The danger of resting in the former is very great in this day, when profession is almost fashionable.

" *August* 30*th.*—I have recently had innumerable proofs of the loving-kindness of my Heavenly Father. On Monday, the 3rd inst., I set out for Bristol with two sisters and two other little girls, and we were graciously preserved through many seen and unseen dangers. In the afternoon we had

a tremendous thunder-storm which continued
with us near twelve miles. The lightning
was exceedingly fierce: once it descended
in a large body of fire in a brake on our
left; the driver and horses were much
frightened, and a solemn awe rested on my
mind. A wheel of the chaise was so much
shattered that we did not expect it would
have held together to our journey's end.
When we got to Okehampton, as we could
not procure a chaise in the town to go on
that night, I embraced the opportunity of
seeking some religious persons. On going
down one street, I called at several houses,
and at last came to the very house where
the Methodist preachers lodged and preached.
I was an entire stranger, but felt great liberty
in speaking to those present of the privilege
of having the Gospel, and the necessity of
accepting salvation as it is offered to us in
the Word of God. The good woman of the
house who was Class-leader,—and the only
person able to conduct prayer-meetings in
the absence of the preacher,—inquired if
I ever spoke in public; as, if I did, she
would let the people know, and gather a

congregation. I told her that I never exercised in any public way, except in cases of
necessity; and that if it were agreeable I
would spend a few minutes in prayer with
her family before I left. So we went upstairs into the little chapel, and the Lord
graciously visited our souls while we were
bowed at His footstool. The day following,
in passing through Cullompton, we met
with great kindness at Mrs. Isaac's, where
I called to inquire for the preacher's family.
We slept that night at Wellington, and the
next day reached Bristol about two o'clock.

"*November 8th.*—During the service this
morning I was greatly blessed. I had
. . . . such animating, encouraging views of
the love, faithfulness and power of God,
as I am at a loss for words to express.
Mr. Drew's discourse on the Divinity of
Christ was truly excellent. I wish I could
see it in print. May it be engraven on my
heart! The lecture which he gave last
Monday evening on the 'Evidences of
Christianity' was also very good.

"*December 6th.*—My dear boy has been
ill. This puts my faith and resignation to

the test.   Very often my fond hopes look
forward; . . . and I am pleased with the
idea of his filling some useful station in the
Church of Christ.   At present appearances
are promising.   His memory is retentive;
he has known all the letters of the alphabet
for a month or two past; he can repeat
several pages of poetry; and he frequently
kneels down to pray, and to thank God
Almighty, as he says, ' for all good things.'

"*April* 18*th*, 1802.—I see the necessity,
and feel resolved, God being my Helper, to
enter into a fresh covenant to devote more of
my time in retirement, to reading, prayer,
self-examination, and meditation.   I know
I have suffered loss through neglect of duty.
Being so much engaged in the world, if I do
not fix on *set times*, something or other is
continually presenting itself as lawful and
needful to be done.   *Any* time is no time.

"*July* 18*th*.—I have lately been passing
through deep waters; and at times have felt
unutterable anguish.   But while the Lord
chastens with the rod He supports with the
staff. . . . . . When I saw my darling boy
sinking into the arms of death, who, who can

describe the agony of my mind? It was worse than tearing flesh from my bones . . . I knew not what to do. I had not removed the dear child from my lap more than five minutes before he ceased to breathe. Just then a calm composure and stayedness of mind on God, stilled the tempest; and I felt I could say, 'Though Thou slay me, yet will I trust in Thee.' Correct views of infinite wisdom and love in His providential dealings towards me, and animating prospects of the glory of the upper and better world, with an assurance of my beloved infant's being in possession of eternal life, bore me above the waves for a season. But soon I felt my own weakness, and was constrained to say, ' Lord, save me ! Lord, help me ! ' and He Who saved sinking Peter stretched out His Almighty hand, and upheld me in the trying hour.

"*August 29th.*—None ever trusted in the Lord and was confounded. No ! His mercy and truth are everlasting. His faithfulness will remain to the latest generation. Glory be to His Name ! He has not forsaken me in adversity; and I have proved

the truth of the promise ' to them that have
no might He increaseth strength.' He has
suffered me to be tried in various ways ;
but these painful seasons have been truly
profitable in weaning my affections from
earth, causing me to trust alone in Jehovah,
giving me to feel the excellency of vital
godliness, and to desire and press after
greater degrees of holiness.   I feel a
measure of love, gratitude, and praise to the
Author of my life, and Giver of every good
and perfect gift ; and I pray that I may be
a living witness of Jesu's power to save even
to the uttermost.   On examination I perceive innumerable wants, two in particular
—*faith*, to lay hold on the promises of God,
and experience their fulfilment; and *humility*,
universal in thought, word, and deed.   I am
prone to cry, ' My leanness ! my leanness !'
and tarry there ; not flying immediately to
the precious blood of Christ—to the rich,
overflowing fountain of boundless love.

"*September* 12*th*.—I have been led to
self-examination, to prove myself whether I
am able to suffer reproaches and injuries—
even for doing those things which I thought

would be most for the glory of God and my soul's profit—without resentment. This seems a difficult attainment. I do not possess it to the full extent. The surest method of ' overcoming evil with good ' is to bear up the offender in the arms of prayer at the throne of grace.

" *September 26th.*—The many tales of woe which I have heard during the past week from various quarters, relative to family trials, have powerfully affected my mind. Surely ' endless is the list of human woes ; and sighs may sooner fail than cause to sigh.' "

During Mrs. Green's widowhood several offers of marriage were firmly declined, and it was not until she felt fully persuaded that it was the will of God that she consented to become the wife of the Rev. Edmund Shaw. The 28th of September, 1802, was the wedding-day. "It was spent," says the bride, "in agreeable conversation, reading, singing and prayer,"—a mode of employing the festal hours far more rational, as well as far more Christian, than that which frequently obtains.

CHAPTER V.

"AN ITINERANT AGAIN."

" When I was a wife the Lord was pleased to bless me in my own soul, and to own my weak endeavours to do good to the souls of others. I was enabled, through Divine grace, to be something more than a private member of His Church ; and, glory be to His Name ! I did not go a warfare at my ' own charges.' As no temporal motive ever did influence my mind, I trust it never will, but that I shall attend to the dictates of the Holy Spirit in every important step in life. I am persuaded I should sin against God were I to choose worldly ease, or honour, or riches, in preference to His cross or the path of self-denial."

Thus Mrs. Shaw wrote some time before her second marriage. And these were the principles which influenced her when she resumed her duties as a minister's wife. Is it any marvel that, as one who knew her well testifies, " she was esteemed and beloved wherever she went "? A true help meet, she not only " looked well to the ways of her household," but she took a lively interest in everything connected with the Church of Christ. Were there sick persons to be visited? She was prepared, as far as possible, to minister to their temporal as well as their spiritual necessities. Was there any new movement to be organized or helped? She was willing to give time, and to put forth effort that it might prove a success. Was a Class left without a Leader? She was ready, when appointed, to take it as her charge, and so to watch over the members as to justify the propriety of the appointment.

The work of a Methodist preacher in the beginning of the century was somewhat different from that of a Methodist preacher now. Saddle-bags were still in fashion; and, in many cases, in order that every part of the wide-spreading Circuit might be visited, it was necessary for the minister to be away from home for weeks together. This was the state of things in the St. Austell Circuit, which, at the time of which I write, extended from Liskeard to St. Mawes. Hence on October 10th, only a few days after the wedding, Mrs. Shaw says, " Yesterday Mr. Shaw set off on the long round. I do not expect to see him again for near three weeks."

The " long round " indeed ! On reading this one can understand why the early preachers were styled " rounders." Brethren now in the succession have surely cause for thankfulness that at least in this respect these latter days are so much better than were those days of " auld lang syne " !

Turning again to the diary, we note how Mrs. Shaw pursued the tenour of her way, exemplifying the Christian spirit, and, as opportunity served, "holding forth the Word of Life."

" St. Austell, *October* 17*th*, 1802.—There is scarcely any duty more necessary— perhaps there are few more difficult—than that of strict self-examination. In this profitable exercise my soul is humbled. Past experience reminds me of the loving-kindness and tender mercies of the Lord vouchsafed towards me when faint and ready to die. And at present stayedness of mind on God leads me to Him as the Fountain, and opens to my view an infinite, eternal fulness in Christ Jesus, over, ever flowing with goodness and truth.

" *October 24th.*—Through the past week I have felt renewed desires to be wholly His, and to walk circumspectly and uprightly before Him. ' I know Whom I have believed.' The inward witness of His Spirit raises me above all doubt. O that infidels would renounce prejudice, and make the trial! Let them prove the faithfulness of our God, and see if He will not verify His promises. Surely they would then gladly throw aside speculative notions for the Divine reality of the Gospel, the blessed experience of Redemption through the Saviour's blood and a title to eternal felicity! I have been favoured with the heart-felt satisfaction of hearing from the lips of a poor wanderer (who has forsaken God for nine years) that she is now willing to return. The '.broken cisterns' have yielded no supplies. Her soul has been starved with husks, while

the bread of life and the fountain of living
waters have been offered freely 'without
money and without price.' O what depth
of mercy and longsuffering! Are not the
daily proofs we have of this sufficient
encouragement for the vilest to return?

"*October* 31st.—My heart has been particularly drawn out in gratitude to God for
His preventing, protecting and enlightening grace; and, while exhorting others to
press forward with diligence, it has proved
quickening to my own soul.

"*December* 12th.—This morning I felt it
good to be at the seven o'clock prayer-
meeting, and during the forenoon God has
graciously visited me with His love and
enlightening grace, giving me a discovery of
my wants and privileges. O blessed Lord!
teach me to know myself, and help me to
love Thee with all my heart.

"*December* 26th.—O when shall I learn
the happy art of depending every moment
upon Him Who alone can strengthen my
weakness and cause those desires which He
has given to be accomplished! Nothing
appears, in my esteem, to be of real worth

when compared with the knowledge and love of God. Nothing is so desirable as to increase in faith and holiness, and to be useful to the immortal souls of our fellow creatures. The more my soul is engaged in these blessed exercises, the more joy and peace do I feel; but the various temporal concerns which necessarily engross my time and attention seem oftentimes to clip my wings, chain me down to earth, and cause me to grovel in the dust. Last Monday, in visiting a poor sick girl, I was peculiarly assisted, both in speaking plainly and affectionately to her, and in praying with her. Yesterday, while visiting a poor man who is very ill, and talking with him about his everlasting concerns, I felt my soul much blessed. These employments are very profitable, and in general bring a present reward.

"*March 6th*, 1803.—In family and private prayer a throne of grace has been accessible. Jesus is 'altogether lovely.'

> 'O what is earth if heaven be mine ?
> And what its dying toys ?
> I seek, I burn, for wealth Divine,
> For God's immortal joys!'

" *March* 27*th.*—My dear sister Mary, about twelve years of age, has obtained a sense of pardoning love. Now all our family have at least their names among the people of God, and I trust are all seeking a ' better country,' as the change from sin and vanity to seriousness and circumspection is evidenced in their conduct.

" *May* 22*nd.*—Last Sunday evening my heart was softened and melted into tears of gratitude on calling to remembrance God's past loving-kindness, and the present mercies which surround me on every side—peace of mind, arising from a consciousness of the Divine favour; evenness of temper, which preserves me, amidst various trying concerns, from being ruffled and unhappy; a good degree of health and strength; kind friends; and all the conveniences of life.

" *May* 29*th.*—Reading à Kempis's 'Christian Pattern,' with prayer and self-examination, has proved very profitable."

During her residence in St. Austell Mrs. Shaw was surrounded by much-loved relatives, and knew nothing of the *res angustæ domi.* But, on her removal to another Circuit, there sprang up fresh experiences, some of them not of the most pleasant kind. These, however, were expected and provided for. A thankful spirit, a cheerful disposition, and the happy art of looking at the bright side of things, and trusting in the living God, she found worth far more to her than ten thousand a year. So, without a fear, without a murmur,—but, on the contrary, with confidence and joy,—a second time she set out from her native place to brave the storms and difficulties which, seventy years ago, Methodist preachers and their families found inseparable from the Itinerancy.

Soon after reaching Redruth, where they were "kindly received by the friends, who appeared much alive to God, and in full expectation of a revival," she wrote :—" I am again become an Itinerant, having left a comfortable habitation, delightful garden, the conveniences of life, relations, etc., for the uncertainties and inconveniences attending this movable state. But, I thank God, I do not seek for honour and riches of an earthly kind. My desire is to lay up my treasure above, and in all things to act in reference to the great Day of Account, when the secret motives of all hearts shall be revealed before assembled worlds."

Mrs. Shaw's feelings and temptations on reaching the new Circuit were somewhat similar to those she had experienced on her arrival at Poole. There was, at first, when engaging in any public work, the same timidity and shrinking as that of which she had written nearly six years before. Hence the following entry:—"At a prayer-meeting, a little way from the town, I was requested to pray. In much fear and trembling I attempted, but did not find free access to the Throne of Grace; and afterwards pride and shame, with various painful feelings, exercised my mind. O when shall I be willing to be anything or nothing—to be despised even for doing what appears right?" But the path of duty is not to be forsaken because it is a rugged path. Satan must not be the victor. Shame must not be allowed to gain the day. So she reasoned, and the result was perseverance in the road marked out for her by the Great Master's hand of love.

CHAPTER VI.

DAYS OF SUNSHINE.

THE charge is sometimes made that biographers are partial; that they do not present a correct, full-length portraiture; that they magnify the excellences, and minify, or altogether overlook, the defects of those respecting whom they write. I am wishful to avoid laying myself open to such a charge; and as the most effectual way of doing this is to allow the subject of our Memoir to speak for herself, I shall continue to give extracts from her diary, only premising that those extracts must, of necessity, be few. A large volume might be filled with selections from her manuscripts, as she jotted down her thoughts and experiences from time to time, even to extreme old age, only laying down her pen when "those that look out of the windows" had become so dim that she could not see to read what she had written.

"Redruth, *December* 22*nd*, 1803.—During the last week I was much tried; but, blessed be God! I do not recollect when I felt so much of the softening influences of Divine grace, or such earnest desires to be like my Blessed Master.

"*January* 4*th*, 1804.—On the 26th ult. the Lovefeast, held after the Quarterly Meeting, was a very remarkable season. The people spoke freely, and, while Mr. Odgers (who was awakened under my ever dear Mr. Green's ministry) was praying, the power of God descended, and my heart was as wax before the fire, ready to receive the impression of my Divine Lawgiver.

"*January* 13*th*.—In the afternoon visited some poor sick people. One old woman was very happy, and sound in her experience. She has been a Methodist for more than fifty years. O what comfort does real religion afford to its possessor in time of trial! The good old saint gave me this charge when we parted,—'Be thou faithful unto death.'

" *July* 15*th.* — At the Lovefeast much blessed while our friends Mr. and Mrs. Odgers were speaking. Never before did I hear such living testimonies of Jesus' power to save to the uttermost; and their consistent conduct is the strongest evidence that they do not ' follow cunningly devised fables.' O how I love uniformity of profession and life ! A remark which Mrs. Odgers made, when conversing with me, I hope I shall never forget. She said :—' I find my happiness does not consist in how much I am beloved by others, but in how well I can exercise this principle towards others on all occasions.' "

Mr. James Odgers, of whom Mrs. Shaw makes affectionate mention, though somewhat eccentric, combined great energy with eminent piety. After having been for several years a Local preacher in the Redruth Circuit, he was sent by the Conference into the Bromsgrove Circuit, and for a quarter of a century he continued to do the work of an Evangelist. In the midst of much opposition and insult, he laboured earnestly and successfully. His wife was one of the

" honourable women " of whom Methodism has had " not a few."

" St. Austell, *July* 22*nd*, 1804.—Yesterday we left Redruth. The piety, love, harmony, and zeal of our excellent people there, together with their kindness and affection, have caused me to feel strong attachment to them. I am thankful that our Heavenly Father has made us the honoured instruments of some good, and that we can rejoice in having seen some fruit of our labours.

" Carmarthen, South Wales, *September* 13*th.*—On Monday morning, August 27th, we left Padstow by the ' Betsey.' The day was delightfully pleasant, and the wind fair. We anchored in Swansea Bay at one o'clock in the morning of the 28th, and at about ten, as soon as the tide served, we got up the river, and landed at Swansea, to my great joy. The following day we set out for Carmarthen. The prospects were fine, but the roads hilly and rough. Since we have been here my earnest desire has been to see Zion in prosperity. At present we are not comfortably situated. No preacher's family

having been here before, we are just break-
ing up fresh ground.

" *December* 23*rd.*—On the 9th our neat
new chapel was opened by Mr. Stanley. I
felt a solemn awe rest on my mind when I
entered the house, with thankfulness that
such a commodious building had been
erected, and that such a large number of
persons of all ranks were assembled to hear
the glad tidings of salvation, and to judge of
the truth for themselves. . . .

" *January* 20*th*, 1805.—Truly ' goodness
and mercy' have 'followed me.' I am now surrounded with favours and privileges which,
if not carefully improved, must surely rise
in judgment against me : kind friends, an
agreeable situation, a good degree of health,
easy circumstances, frequent opportunities
for assembling with the people of God, etc.
O for a thankful, loving, obedient heart!
Teach me, O Thou Who art the Hope and
Saviour of Israel, to walk in Thee, the Way,
the Truth and the Life. Make me a living,
fruitful branch in Thyself, Who art the living
and true Vine. May I live above the perishing trifles of sense, having all my soul spirit-

ualized, all within and without regulated by
Divine grace, and feelingly alive to every
good.

"Haverford-West, *August* 18*th*.—Through
the tender mercy of a kind and gracious
Providence we arrived here safe and well
on Tuesday evening last. May I be enabled
henceforward to 'grow in grace' and in conformity to Jesus, my living Head!

" *October* 13*th*.—Mr. R. came on the 4th.
His preaching is clear, Scriptural and per-
suasive. He is deservedly much esteemed,
and, I trust, will be rendered very useful.
This morning, while he was discoursing on
the Apostle's low views of himself, and
exalted views of his office,—being commis-
sioned to preach ' the unsearchable riches of
Christ,'—I was both pleased and profited.

" *April* 13*th*, 1806.—My outward path
has lately been particularly smooth and
peaceful in every respect. Its duration I
leave to Him Who knows what is best, and
cannot err. O may I diligently pursue my
high calling's prize, and while endeavouring
to urge others on in the narrow path, and
pointing them to an all-sufficient Saviour,

may I *feel* and *do* what I say. Ever blessed
God! teach me to keep my own vineyard,
lest it be overrun with briers and thorns,
and the fences, which have hitherto preserved it, be broken down.

"*May* 11*th.*—Blessed be God! I can praise
Him for a thankful heart, that tastes His
gifts with joy. The reading of my dear
friend Mrs. Stanley's experience, in the
Magazine for this month, has been a blessing to my soul. I feel my own nothingness
and shortcomings, but am enabled to rejoice
in a humbling sense of my poverty, that
Christ may be all in all.

"*June* 1*st.*—After the evening preaching
we held a Love-feast. Jesus Himself drew
near, and refreshed the weary, hungry souls
with the Bread of Life. The time was fully
employed by the numerous witnesses who
were ready to declare, from the fulness of
their hearts, what God had done for their
souls. Timid and backward as I am, I could
not withhold my testimony of His mercy,
truth and faithfulness.

"*June* 15*th.*—Yesterday I visited Pembroke with my dear husband. Pembroke

G

is pleasantly situated. The society is pious, simple and affectionate. I should like it very well as a place of residence, if obliged to relinquish my beloved itinerant life.

"Stroud, *September* 7th.—On the 12th ult. we received our appointment to this place, and with much sorrow and regret we have left our much-loved and kind friends at Haverford-West. May the blessings of peace, unity and prosperity ever attend them! I am pleased with the situation here, and trust the Lord will abundantly revive His work in poor, dull Stroud.

"*October* 5th.—On Saturday Mr. R. arrived from Cornwall, and on Tuesday last I accompanied my sister to the church, where the marriage ceremony was performed, with great reverence, by the pious Mr. Williams. To-day I have been blessed with a spirit of importunity in praying for my children, and asking wisdom from above to guide them aright, and to act agreeably to the Divine will in all things."

The "Mr. R." here referred to was the Rev. Thomas Rogers, who, "after he had served his own generation by the will of God," " with faith unshaken, hope without a cloud, and love which knows no fear, ' fell on sleep' at St. Austell on July 9th, 1864." At the time of his death he was the oldest minister in the Wesleyan-Methodist Connexion. For forty years his career was one of active usefulness; and when obliged to become a Supernumerary, he continued, as strength permitted, to prosecute his much-loved work, till at length extreme bodily exhaustion brought his labours to an end. His beloved wife, who lived to fourscore years, was the oldest half-sister of Mrs. Shaw. " All through her long life," writes one who knew her well, " she conducted her domestic affairs in a most exemplary manner, and as a wife, a mother, and a mistress, was a pattern of all that is excellent."

" *April 26th*, 1807.—I believe God is infinite in all His perfections, and wise and good in all His dispensations. When He trieth us it is for our profit and in mercy. A little more than a fortnight since our valuable servant, my dear Mary, was taken ill, and on Monday last I was under the painful necessity of parting with her. I have felt it to be a grievous trial, as so much of our domestic comfort depends on a good servant. But this gives me another opportunity of exercising resignation and faith.

"*June* 14*th.*—Last Tuesday our neat chapel at Painswick was opened by Mr. James Wood, from Bristol. His deep, solid, unaffected piety added weight to his excellent discourses.

"*June* 28*th.*—On Monday last my dear husband and I walked to Renwick's Ash, where we had one of the most beautiful, extensive and varied prospects I ever beheld. On returning to the village, Renwick, I accepted an invitation from a poor woman to go in and sit down, and had a favourable opportunity of speaking to her on the importance of salvation from sin and its consequences.

"*July* 12*th.*—Visited many of the poor and sick, who all agree in their testimony that 'before they were afflicted they went astray.'

"*October* 25*th.*—As to outward things, my

cup is full and running over. My domestic sweets are as many as fall perhaps to the share of any individual. 'Bless the Lord, O my soul, and forget not all His benefits!'

"*November* 15*th.*—This morning when I awoke these words occupied my attention: 'The Lord redeemeth the soul of His servants; and none of them that trust in Him shall be desolate.' How full! Blessed be His name! I can set to my seal that He is true. He hath redeemed me from innumerable evils, and from the fear of death, and by trusting in Him my mind is preserved in peace.

"*December* 20*th.*—Never did I feel as I have of late such a renunciation of self, and such a giving up of body, soul and all that is dear to me to my all-wise and gracious God. I am happily freed from painful forebodings and anxious care. All is peace. How multiplied are the mercies I enjoy!

"*February* 28*th*, 1808.—Temptations have at times so powerfully oppressed me that I have been constrained to cry unto the Lord to undertake for me. He has delivered and doth still deliver me. Some time in January I attended the funeral of that eminent servant of God, the Rev. Cornelius Winter, at Painswick. May my end be like his!

"*April* 17*th.*—I feel it good to live with eternity in view, and to commit myself and all my concerns into His gracious hands Who cannot fail to do what is best for me and with me. O for a more lively faith and a more obedient love!

"*May* 29*th.*—Blessed be His name! God has been with me, and often refreshed my soul with Divine consolations. He has made bare His arm; and, contrary to all human probability, raised me from the margin of the grave. O may I live to love and praise Him!

"*June* 19*th.*—Various circumstances have afforded opportunities for exercising Christian tempers and manifesting dispositions which grow not in nature's garden. Often have I been led to study the example of our Blessed Master, and then to examine my own heart and life to see how nearly they correspond with His. For ever be His name

adored Who has been my joy in grief, my
strength in weakness, my light in darkness,
and Who has helped me so that I have not
fainted in the day of adversity!

" Camelford, *September* 11*th.*—When we
arrived here, I was agreeably disappointed
in our habitation; for, though it is small,
inconvenient, old and poor, yet such had
been my ideas, from the various descriptions
given, that it is better than I expected. ' The
best of all is, God is with us.' To-day, while
reading St. John xiv. 23, I thought I never
before saw so much beauty and excellency in
it. The promise so full: what can a soul
possibly desire more?

" *February 5th,* 1809.—Numerous family
engagements, increased by the slowness and
thoughtlessness of a giddy, good-tempered
servant, with bodily indisposition, have
hindered me from doing as I otherwise
would. Still, to the honour of my gracious
God would I say that He has been a ' very
present help' in the time of need. In general,
my mind has enjoyed calm, settled peace,
and I have been blessed with enlargement in
prayer. I often lament my want of more

patience and real composure in teaching the dear children, and bearing with their follies and weaknesses, their perverseness and self-will.

" *March* 19*th.*—I feel peculiarly called at present to the exercise of those graces of the Spirit which are hid from public view.

" *May* 14*th.*—The soul-animating principle of Divine love in the heart raises us above transitory things, and, in proportion to our love, so will our faith be in exercise in the precious promises which are all ' Yea and Amen ' in Christ Jesus. The account of Mr. Haslam, with the extracts from his diary, published in the Magazine, have been rendered truly profitable. How have I longed to imitate that man of God in acquiring self-knowledge, humility, supreme love to God, zeal for the salvation of immortal souls, diligence and usefulness! but I feel I am nothing.

" *August* 13*th.* — During this time of general anxiety to Methodists, especially to the preachers and their families, I have felt it good to trust in the Lord, and to pray that He would fix our appointment where it may be most for His glory and our spiritual improvement.

" *October* 22*nd.*—Mr. Drew has visited us this week, and preached two excellent sermons."

Mr. Drew was for many years a highly esteemed friend of Mrs. Shaw's. At the time she wrote, he was already extensively known as the author of several valuable works. " He combined," writes the late Dr. Etheridge, " much of the dialectical acumen of a Plato, with much of the evangelic grace of a St. John." For an example of what indomitable perseverance, in the midst of mountain difficulties, can accomplish, perhaps no one can do better than study the Life of Samuel Drew, M.A., who rose from a lowly position to become one of the foremost literary men of his day. Methodists should not willingly let his name and memory die.

CHAPTER VII.

SHADOWS ON THE WAY.

" CAMELFORD, *December* 24*th*, 1809.—I think it an unspeakable favour, calculated to promote my highest interests, that my generally smooth path has some rough places in it. On a dangerous road we walk more cautiously, and take heed to our ways; but when all seems smooth and even, we walk on regardless of any snares that might cause our fall or destruction.

"*April 8th*, 1810.—The Lord has heard the prayers of His people for the revival of His work. Many, young and old, backsliders and others, are apparently athirst for salvation through Jesus Christ. The Classes are now very large, and several persons have spoken to me about taking one: indeed, two or three say if I will lead a Class they will come. The importunity and advice of pious friends have vanquished my fears

and objections, and I have consented to begin
next Wednesday. May the Lord be my wisdom
and strength !

" *June 3rd.*—To-day our beautiful new
chapel has been opened by Mr. Waddy and
my dear brother, Mr. Rogers. I think it is
altogether the prettiest and most complete
of any I have yet seen. The Lord has graciously blessed the endeavours of His servants
in this good work, and peace and unity pre-
vail among us.

" *Tuesday, July 31st.*—I took a ride with
a few friends to see Row-tor and Dosmary
Pool. I was astonished to behold such im-
mense rocks placed one on another to so great
a height. Though my head is weak, yet, with
some assistance, I climbed to the topmost,
and discovered many hollows and troughs,
evidently executed by human hands, though
the design is unknown. After feasting our
eyes with the delightful scenery which presented itself on all sides, we dined on the
rocks, and then proceeded to the Pool, a
beautiful sheet of water, nearly three miles
in circumference. On one side the white
sand, which is washed up from time to time,

looks similar to the beach near the sea. One
thing which attracted our notice at Row-
tor was some beautiful moss, which grew
in a dark, wet cave, and produced a light
like that arising from a number of glow-
worms. On touching it, it became dull,
and of a very dark green. These grand
views of nature raised my thoughts to the
great Author. On the whole, it was a profitable day.

"Ashburton, *November 6th.*—My dear husband's ministry is more than usually successful. Some chapels are so crowded that
there is not room for the people. What is
still better than large congregations, very
many are seeking redemption in Jesus, so
that the fields are white to the harvest. On
the 19th ult. I received the affecting account that my very dear father's departure
was at hand, and on the following morning we set out for St. Austell, where, on
arriving the same night, we heard of his
death. On the Sunday morning I followed
his remains to the church, where the funeral
service was blessed to me; and the hymn,
'Again we lift our voice,' etc., sung by our

Methodist singers, was delightful. In the evening Mr. S. Drew addressed the largest congregation I ever saw in St. Austell chapel from Hosea xiii. 14 :—' I will ransom them,' etc.—an excellent discourse, in which he gave an impartial and satisfactory account of my dear father.

" *June 2nd*, 1811.—The late gracious inter-position of Providence with respect to the suppression of Lord Sidmouth's Bill, and the opposition made, or intended to be made, to it by our beloved Sovereign, caused sensations which I cannot describe. No temporal loss or gain ever so affected me as the fear of losing our religious privileges.*

" *February 9th*, 1812.—During the past week I have been much profited in reading Baxter's ' Dying Thoughts.' At times my mind has been painfully exercised from a

---

* Had Lord Sidmouth's obnoxious Bill " For ex-plaining and rendering more effectual certain Acts relating to Protestant Dissenting Ministers " been adopted, it would have been to a great extent sub-versive of the religious liberties of the people, and must have abridged the privileges of the Methodists, and hindered them in their good work. Happily,

fear that I do not possess that degree of heavenly-mindedness which would make heaven heaven to me. . . . . But, blessed be God! on examination I think I can say I endeavour to keep the end in view, and wish to do all in reference to the great Day of Account. I would not knowingly or willingly offend God. The pamphlet alluded to has afforded me strong consolation on this head, and throughout it has tended to quicken my desires and raise my affections heavenward. What a privilege to be favoured with time, opportunity and inclination for reading! Who can tell its advantages or know its value? None who have not a taste for it. I lament that so much of my time has been lost that might have been improved. At present I am very favourably situated in a quiet, peaceful habitation. I am not a slave to visiting, which murders so much of our

---

the whole Connexion was aroused, Dissenters generally united in denouncing the coercive measure, petitions were poured into the House of Lords, remonstrance followed remonstrance ; and although Lord Sidmouth refused to withdraw the Bill, on the second reading, May 21st, 1811, it was rejected without a division.

time in some Circuits. Though our kind
friends mean well, and in some instances it
may be profitable, yet, in general, it is much
to be feared, that many evils are consequent
upon the frequent practice of it. It dissi-
pates the mind, prevents us from attending
with that regularity to stated times of devotion which we can maintain at home, and in-
terrupts the order necessary to be preserved
in our families if we wish to secure comfort.
Consistency of character and the Christian
temper are finely drawn in that entertain-
ing and instructive work entitled 'Cælebs
in Search of a Wife.' And the power of religion to support the mind under trying circumstances, and stimulate to active obedience
is prettily represented in the history of Widow
Placid in 'An Antidote to the Miseries of
Human Life.' These works will afford amuse-
ment and instruction. I have lately read
them with pleasure.

"*March* 1st.—I have been enabled to possess my soul in patience in a good degree
amidst some trying scenes. When a person
offered to spit in my face for my 'imperti-
nence,' I was able to bear the insult with-

out being much agitated, and without feeling anger. This arose only from urging the importance of attending the means of grace.

"Tavistock, *November* 1st.—We came to this place on August 24th, across Dartmoor, and called to see the French prison by the way. My mind has been painfully exercised of late in seeing my dear husband so much indisposed. . . . . How many little exercises have I had from the children, servants, etc. These seem to make up by their number and variety what they individually want in weight. I have to-day felt the need of exercising a Christian temper.

"*February* 21st, 1813.—The cause of Methodism here is promising. The congregations are large and attentive, and a few are inquiring the way to Zion, with their faces thitherward. Many of our friends pressed and urged their request so hard that, though very reluctant, I began meeting a Female Class about three weeks since. Fearing to omit an opportunity which might prove useful to others, and considering that I had only one life to live, and that it would soon end, when no more work could be done, I took up the cross. I trust this feeble attempt to serve the interest of my God and Saviour will be blessed and owned by Him.

"*April* 17*th*, 1814.—Last Sunday morning we were informed of the joyful tidings of Peace. The event being unexpected, it seemed too much to be true; but this week it has been confirmed. I would say, 'Bless the Lord, O my soul : and all that is within me, bless His holy name.' Now, Lord, ride on conquering and to conquer till the earth is filled with Thy glory!

"Brixham, *March* 5*th*, 1815.—This day fortnight, while thinking on the missionaries who are gone to distant lands to preach 'the unsearchable riches of Christ,' I felt my heart drawn out in prayer to God for success in their labours, and resolved to set forward a female society for their support. I mentioned this to a friend, who promised her help, and we have a few names on our paper. Though the beginning be small, may it increase more and more. The letters lately received from Ceylon contain such interesting accounts, that tears of gratitude to God

H

for the displays of His goodness and mercy
to His servants caused me frequently to stop
while I was perusing them.   Though their
venerable friend, Dr. Coke, was taken suddenly from them, yet Almighty God, in this
instance, has shown that He is *God all-
sufficient*, that He can supply—yea, far more
than supply—the place of any of His creatures.

The Mission cause was then in its infancy.
The progress made in a few years had been,
it is true, very remarkable, especially in
Nova Scotia and the West Indies ; and yet,
apart from these, the few agents of the
Society had but made a beginning.   At the
Conference of 1815 the number of members
returned from the Mission Stations in
Europe, Asia and Africa showed a total
of only 270 ; and the whole sum raised
for Mission-purposes did not amount to
£10,000.   It would be interesting to review
the progress made by the Society during the
many years in which it was Mrs. Shaw's
delight to work for and contribute to its
funds. This, however, is beyond our province.

Suffice it to say, that it had a place in her affections as long as she lived. She had listened to Dr. Coke's earnest appeals in behalf of the West Indies. She had wept over his sudden removal from the little company of young Evangelists who seemed so dependent on him. She felt that special effort would be needed now that the Father of our Missions was gone, and she was determined, the Lord being her Helper, to do what she could. As year followed year, she gratefully noted the success with which God blessed His servants' labours; and with loving heart, and in the spirit of self-sacrifice, she continued to present her free-will offerings and her prayers. It was her delight in after years, while residing at St. Austell, to show hospitality to those who took part in the Annual Missionary Services. The time of the Anniversary was to her a season of pleasant activity and excitement as the following extract from a letter testifies :—

" May 14th, 1851.

" We have lately had our Missionary Anniversary. Our deputation were the Revs.

W. L. Thornton and David Hay, of London,
and Levi Waterhouse, from Falmouth.
George Smith, Esq., from Camborne, was
our chairman.   A very blessed, hallowing
influence pervaded all the services, and the
collections were upwards of £14 more than
last year.   I was not able to attend any of
the services, except the Breakfast Meeting,
on the Tuesday morning, which was a delightful opportunity.   The weather was cold, with
showers of snow and hail, which made it
unfavourable for an early attendance; yet
we had a very respectable number present.   Though I had been unwell, I was so
far restored as to be able to get through
the fatigues of the busy time.   I always
account it a privilege and honour to be
so circumstanced as to be able to entertain the servants of the Lord on such an
occasion."

When, in consequence of the infirmities of
age, Mrs. Shaw could no longer attend the
Anniversary Services, her interest continued
unabated, and at each Annual Meeting her
subscription was forthcoming, accompanied

with a short note. The last she wrote, dated
April 12th, 1871, is as follows:—

" Through the tender mercies of our
Heavenly Father, I am enabled once more
to contribute my trifle to the cause which
lies near my heart, praying that the seed
may take root and bear fruit, not only a
hundred, but a thousand fold. . . . Enclosed
is 21s. from

" ELIZABETH SHAW."

CHAPTER VIII.

A NIGHT OF SORROW.

"My thoughts are not your thoughts, neither are your ways my ways, saith the Lord."

Certain passages in the life of Mrs. Shaw indicate the truthfulness of the Lord's words.

However it may be accounted for, it is the fact that many of the most devoted followers of Christ have found parts of the road to the "pearly gates" rough and thorny in the extreme. By the hand of their Father God they have been led

"A way no more expected
Than when His sheep Passed through the deep,
By crystal walls protected."

Some few have experienced tribulation all the journey through, and life has been to them one long, unbroken chapter of sorrow. They hoped for years of activity; they have had years of painful, inactive waiting instead. Others have had here and there to tread the wild. Ever and anon their weary feet have bled, and their soul has been " discouraged because of the way." They have met with *Marahs* as well as *Elims;* and there have been alternations of songs and sighs, of gladness and grief. The bright yesterday has been followed by the dark to-day—the joyous *Then* by the saddening *Now.*

Thus it was with Mrs. Shaw. There were times when she could write of the cup of blessing, "full and running over," and of "domestic sweets, as many as fall perhaps to the share of any individual." There were other times when she felt ready to utter the Psalmist's wail, "O my God, my soul is cast down within me. . . . . Deep calleth unto deep at the noise of Thy waterspouts all Thy waves and Thy billows are gone over me!" (Ps. xlii. 6, 7.) And such a time was that when, in 1815, circumstances arose which compelled her to relinquish her "beloved itinerant life." But her Journal testifies that even then, and during several subsequent years of anxiety, she never mis-

trusted the wisdom and goodness of her God.
When everything appeared to be against her,
and those she loved most fondly, she held
fast her confidence.   When investments
proved unremunerative, and capital gradually
diminished; when trusted *employés* were
found to be incompetent and untrustworthy;
when on the farm account and on the
shipping account the balance was again and
again on the wrong side; when loss followed
loss until well-nigh all was gone, and there
was the prospect of penury, she remained
steadfast, still "looking unto Jesus," the
hand still working for Him, and the heart
still confiding in Him.   Indeed, Mrs. Shaw
found—with what saint has it been otherwise?—that the time of sore trial was a time
of great blessing.   As precious metals after
having passed through the furnace become
more precious, and as fragrant flowers when
crushed become more fragrant, so, in our
friend's case, "the trial of faith" brought
her nearer to Christ, and produced a beneficial
effect upon her throughout the remainder
of her days.   In the midst of her suffering she had peace, and was able to "commit

the keeping " of her soul to God " in well doing, as unto a faithful Creator." Turning to the diary, we note the faith, the calmness and the " patience of hope " which were manifest in the day of trouble.

" Ferry's Hall, near Buckfastleigh, *March* 17*th*, 1816.—At the Class-meeting I have often found my soul watered and refreshed with the dew from on high ; and also in reading Mason's excellent little work on ' Self-Knowledge.' The promises in the Scriptures have oftentimes been the comfort and support of my fainting, drooping spirits ; but I cannot recollect when they have been more precious than on the last Sunday and the week preceding. When my foreboding fears have anticipated unutterable things, this Word has been as an anchor to my soul, ' Thou shalt be far from oppression ; for thou shalt not fear : and from terror ; for it shall not come near thee.'

" *March* 31*st*.—I wish to commit body, soul and spirit into His hands Who has hitherto been my Helper, and Whose 'grace is sufficient,' let what will befall me, if I am found trusting in Him.

" *July 7th.*—'The mercy of the Lord is from everlasting to everlasting upon them that fear Him;' and in this He enables me to confide. He graciously vouchsafes to comfort and refresh my soul, from time to time, with such views of His Providential care, Almighty power and goodness as are calculated to increase my faith and trust in Him. On Friday week my dear brother, Mr. Rogers, visited us. On the Sunday I ventured to go to chapel, and my dear infant was baptized *Samuel.* The text was: 'And did all eat the same spiritual meat; and did all drink the same spiritual drink: for they drank of that spiritual Rock that followed them: and that Rock was Christ.' (1 Cor. x. 3, 4.) It was indeed to my soul 'a feast of fat things,' and though I lament my want of memory to retain those excellent and important truths, yet I bless the Lord for the refreshing influences of His Spirit which I received, and which still afford a savour of what I heard.

" *April 13th,* 1817.—I am again permitted to recount the mercies of God in preserving me from danger and accident during my late journey into Cornwall. While at St. Austell, the Quarterly Meeting was held there. Many bore a blessed testimony for Jesus, and were enabled to say that His blood cleansed from all sin: among others, a young man, Walter Lawry, who is going as missionary to New Holland.

" *December 7th.*—This day fortnight I was so filled with love, gratitude and praise to God for His goodness as to be compelled to kneel down and pour out my full heart in unutterable thanksgiving to Him. This morning also I felt my heart drawn out after God, praising Him for His multiplied mercies, and desiring an increase of spiritual-mindedness and devotedness to Him. O may all our steps be guided by His unerring wisdom; and in all our straits, perplexities and trials may we prove that 'all things work together for good'!

" *March 29th*, 1818.—I do not remember when I have passed such a blessed week as this past has been. My soul has been drawn out in strong desires for an increase of spiritual light and life, and a more constant possession of all the graces of the Spirit.

Clearer light has shone on my mind respecting the nature of justifying faith. I have been greatly blessed in reading Mrs. Fletcher's Life. I fully coincide with her views respecting the knowledge which our dear departed friends have of our concerns below, and the deep communion which is sometimes permitted between them and us . . . . I never met with anything before so exactly descriptive of what I have felt.

"*April 26th.*—Since reading Mrs. Fletcher's Life, I have read M. De Renty's. His deep communion with God, burning zeal, fervent charity and profound humility cause me to feel self-abasement before Him who searcheth the heart. May I derive spiritual advantage from the many privileges with which I am favoured!

"*June 21st.*—Mrs. H. A. Rogers' Experience and Letters have been much blessed to me, and amidst all my trials I have been borne above them, believing that, as it respects myself, all will be well.

'Thy every act pure blessing is,
Thy path unsullied light.'

"*April 25th*, 1819.—It appears as though

God had directed our steps in a temporal way, differently from what we had designed. May all our concerns be under His all-wise direction and influence! Perhaps, in more than twenty instances have our plans been frustrated; and though we have keenly felt the disappointments, yet I bless the Lord that in the midst of them all I have been enabled to trust in Him."

About this time the harassed ones had some thought of leaving England and settling in America, but this project, like others to which reference has been made, came to nothing. At first Mrs. Shaw objected to the proposal, but, on further consideration, she changed her views, and felt willing to go. Why the scheme was given up does not appear.

"*July* 11*th*, 1819.—I now feel quite free from those fears and anxieties respecting a voyage across the Atlantic which so much haunted me a while ago; and were I to choose, I think I should prefer going with my family. I pray that infinite Wisdom and

Goodness may direct all our steps. O my God! use me as an instrument in Thine hand to promote Thy cause, and to glorify Thy name wherever my lot may be cast.

" *August 8th.*—I am become quite decided respecting emigration to America, and were it to depend only on myself, I should not hesitate at all. The more I think on such a step, the more fully I approve.

" *September 5th.*—I have felt a strong desire to get Fletcher's Appeal, Alleine's Alarm, and Baxter's Call, purposely to lend to persons who might be disposed to read them. As I had laid aside a few shillings some time since, which were given me to be used in any necessitous way, I thought they could not be better employed than in the purchase of these works.

" *November 9th.* — The first Methodist chapel ever built at Teignmouth was opened to-day by Messrs. Buckley and Bryant. May many precious souls be brought to God there!

" Brixham, *March 12th*, 1820.—Trials and perplexities have driven me to a throne of grace. Here is my only place of refuge.

"*April* 9*th.*—My soul longeth for an indwelling God, and an entire conformity to Jesus. Last Sunday my husband and I partook of the Sacrament of the Lord's Supper. Our minds have been painfully exercised; but my requests have been made known unto God, with thanksgiving for past mercies and deliverances.

"*April* 30*th.*—The second perusal of Mrs. Fletcher's Life has been greatly blessed to me. I feel assured that God is infinitely wise and good in chastening us, and that we shall have cause to praise Him to all eternity, and 'most for the severe.'

"*June* 11*th.*—I have been entreated to take the charge of Mr. L.'s Monday Class. The members are so attached to their leader that no other will, I fear, be acceptable; yet he particularly wishes me to take it. O my God! if Thou hast appointed this charge for me, give me favour in the eyes of the people, and grant me humility, love, zeal and faithfulness in the solemn, important and arduous work assigned me.

"*July* 16*th.*—Our increasing trials constrain me to depend on my Almighty, all-sufficient Saviour, and, glory be to His name! not in vain.   Last Sunday morning I awoke with these words, which have been much on my mind since then :—

> ' Blind unbelief is sure to err,
>   And scan His work in vain ;
> God is His own Interpreter,
>   And He will make it plain.'

And in prayer I seldom omit these lines :—

> ' Use the rod and not the sword,
>   Correct with kind severity ;
> Bring me not to nothing, Lord,
>   But bring me home to Thee.'

" *August* 13*th.*—I have often thought of a saying frequently used by my late dear mother, ' God cannot trust me with a day's health : my heart is so treacherous, I am prone to forget Him and wander from Him.' This is too much the case with me.   When my outward circumstances are smooth and promising, I do not so sensibly feel my dependence on God, nor that exercise of faith in His promises, as when oppressed with cares and trials."

CHAPTER IX.

THE FAITHFUL TEACHER.

In the beginning of the year 1821 Mrs. Shaw undertook the responsible and important work of instructing a few pupils, a position for which both by gifts and grace she was well fitted, and in which she met with much that could not fail to bring gladness to her heart. Gradually the numbers increased, so that in 1823 it was thought desirable to remove from Brixham to larger premises at Buckfastleigh. Not only had Mrs. Shaw the satisfaction of seeing those under her care advancing in knowledge and greatly attached to herself, but what gave her even more joy, she saw many of them yield themselves to God and His Church, and join the Class of which she was Leader. From her voluminous journal I select the following entries, written during the years in which she continued the school:—

I

"Brixham, *April* 29*th*, 1821.—On Sunday I began writing a few outlines of the way in which the Lord has graciously led me through the wilderness. I have often thought of doing it, and many friends have urged it, but I do not feel any liberty in proceeding with it to-day.

"*May* 13*th*.—I visited the poor-house on Thursday. There were nearly twenty who assembled, apparently with a desire to receive some good. I read two chapters, sang and prayed with them, and felt much freedom in talking to them; and also, on my return, in speaking to a poor backslider. O Lord, Thou canst use the meanest instrument to accomplish Thy purposes! Make bare Thine arm and rescue these souls from the power of the deceiver!

"*June* 10*th*.—Truly 'my soul thirsteth for God, for the living God'! O when shall I wake up after His likeness, and be satisfied with His fulness? It is cause for increasing gratitude that my ardour does not diminish, but that my desires after God and the salvation of my fellow immortals are renewed. How true is it that they who water shall be

watered! The other week I engaged to call
on some persons to get something towards
the Missionary Fund. In this noble cause
my heart is engaged; and from early youth
I have thought if I were a man, and endued
with ministerial talents, how gladly would
I go even to the ends of the earth to make
known ' the unsearchable riches of Christ' to
a perishing world. In this new employment
various emotions agitated me. Some wished
me success, and gave a trifle. Others, from
different motives, withheld their aid and
availed themselves of some paltry excuse
for saving their pockets; but, alas! what
account will they give of their stewardship
when called to the bar of God?

"*June* 20*th.*—Received a letter from my
dear Edmund, giving a pleasing account
of many of the boys at Kingswood being
convinced of sin, and at a prayer-meeting,
held on Whit-Monday, finding peace. May
my dear William be among the number of
those brought to a saving knowledge of the
truth as it is in Jesus!

"*August* 12*th.*—'Tis easy to talk of faith,
patience and resignation, but these graces

can only be known to be genuine when . . .
put to the test.

" *September* 30*th*.—I feel my heart grieved
in seeing and hearing of the prevalence
of conformity to the world in dress among
the Methodists. I fear it argues want of
piety, a departure from Christian simplicity,
a disregard to the unerring Word of Truth
and a love of this present evil world. . . . O
that they would rise superior to these frivo-
lous vanities, and discover true greatness of
mind by denying themselves and taking up
and bearing the cross! Were we always to
act in reference to eternity and the great
Day of Account, would there be such waste
of time and money and such insensibility to
the claims of the pious poor, the cause of
God and the perishing heathen? O my God,
save me, I beseech Thee, from the general
contagion, and help me to bear my feeble
testimony against that which appears to me
so replete with mischief!

" *February* 3*rd*, 1822.—Many of our neighbours and friends have been lately called
away from a state of trial to their eternal
home. All the sympathies of my nature

have been called into exercise in visiting the dying and the bereaved families I have lately seen.

"*May* 19*th.*—I have been reading the Life of that truly excellent woman Lady Maxwell, with much pleasure and profit. It is highly encouraging and animating to learn how they fought and conquered; how they sought and obtained strength, grace and glory who were encompassed with the same trials and difficulties as we are who are now engaged in the warfare.

"Buckfastleigh, *August* 17*th*, 1823.—Soon after we came here Mr. Sanders sent me a Class-paper, published from the pulpit that there would be a Class-meeting the next evening, and invited any who desired to save their souls and to unite themselves with us to be there. I am thankful to find that six or seven seem sincerely desirous of joining with us in the pursuit of eternal life.

"*April* 10*th*, 1825.—Blessed be God! I have felt my heart more drawn after Him this day. From the time I awoke this morning these lines have been in my thoughts,—

> ' Since nothing can be good for me,
>   However pleasant it may be,
>   That is displeasing Lord to Thee,
>   May I dislike it too.'

" *June* 12*th.*—On the 19th ult. my dear
Edmund and Elizabeth accompanied me to
Plymouth, and the next morning we sailed
from Stonehouse to Fowey in the steam-
packet. Our passage was rough, owing to
a brisk easterly wind, but we were not more
than two hours and forty minutes in going
the thirty miles. I was preserved from fear
though not from sickness. These words of
Mr. Olivers' were much on my mind,—

> ' The watery deep I pass
>   With Jesus in my view.'

While at Fowey, past seasons, when I have
poured out my heart before God and have
obtained promises and encouragement, were
brought fresh to my remembrance. In visiting a poor, afflicted woman, who is confined
to her bed in a little room not more at most
than six feet square, with the window closed,
except a little hole or two which she had
made to admit light to enable her to read
her Bible, I was unusually blessed. By the

power of Divine grace she could rejoice in God her Saviour without murmuring; and I felt free access to the throne while praying with her.

" While visiting Mr. H. Roberts, of Plymouth, I could not but approve and admire his conduct. When near seven o'clock he said, ' My friends, I hope you will make yourselves comfortable, and that I shall find you all here on my return; but, as it is my Class-night, I must ask you to excuse me for an hour.' O that this firmness, this conscientious regard to the worship and honour of God were more generally manifested by all professors!

" *June 26th.*—Last Sunday my dear husband preached three times. He appeared to be favoured with the unction from on high. His ministry is highly esteemed and very profitable. I feel a grateful heart for innumerable mercies, and confidence ' for all that's to come.'

" *September 4th.*—I must be firm in improving the time and devoting more of it to reading. 'Tis true I have numerous things to attend to, and am constantly employed from early in the morning till late at night, but how will all these apparently necessary duties appear when I am called to give an account of my stewardship if I have omitted the more important concerns of feeding the soul with spiritual food? I have never neglected reading my Bible daily when alone; but I have been almost insensibly drawn away from my former practice of reading something else which was calculated to inform, strengthen, quicken and animate my soul in the pursuit of eternal realities.

" *September* 11*th*.—Last Sunday I felt my mind in a very blessed state: all fear of death removed, and strong confidence in God as my Friend and Portion. On Monday evening I walked into Ashburton to hear Rowland Hill. I was agreeably disappointed. He was serious, plain and practical in a very high degree. He appeared to have attained to a high state of holiness in his own experience; and the fervour and heavenly-mindedness which he evinced deeply affected my mind, which was in a prepared state to receive those divine truths which dropped from his lips. His text was: ' Seeing ye have purified your souls in obeying the truth through the Spirit unto unfeigned love of the brethren, see that ye love one another with a pure heart fervently.' (1 Pet. i. 22.)

",*September* 18*th.*—I would praise the Lord with my whole heart for His goodness manifested to my children. Four out of the seven are members of Society, and I trust are sincerely following Christ.

" *May* 14*th*, 1826.—I am fully aware that the generality of professors do not live under the influence of Bible truths [as it is their privilege to do]. Were we to receive a letter from a faithful friend, whose kindness we had often experienced, assuring us that he was going to send us certain remittances by such and such a conveyance, should we doubt it? Should we not fully expect and make the needful inquiries about them? But where is the person who takes God at His word and believes he shall receive what God has promised to send? O how awfully and deeply are we fallen! how has sin blinded our eyes and hardened our hearts! Pardon my ingratitude and unbelief, O Lord, for Jesus' sake!

"*May* 21*st.*—It affords me hope and encouragement when I discover in the minds of the children any feeling or concern respecting their salvation.   This day fortnight Mr. Shaw preached : and in the evening, while talking to them, I observed deeper attention, and their hearts more softened. While I was at supper, Miss P. came to me and requested I would come up and pray with them.   I gladly complied with the request, and found them all in tears.   May the impressions be deep and lasting !

"*December* 31*st.*—Glory and praise be ascribed to God for the innumerable mercies and favours He has bestowed on me and mine during the year that is now nearly closed.   Three of my children have stepped into Gospel liberty . . . in addition to two others who were partakers of the blessing before. . . . O Lord, bless and save all my children to the very uttermost !

"*February* 18*th*, 1827.—Last Tuesday two more of our young ladies earnestly requested to be allowed to go to the Class-meeting, and appear very sincere and desirous to devote themselves to God.   Two others, who have met for some time, have obtained pardon. The rest appear to like good things. O that they may be all taught of God!

"*May 20th.*—I trust my feeble efforts in lending tracts and talking to the children who borrow them will be made a blessing.

"*July 8th.*—I have recently visited Cornwall. At Fowey I was delighted to find my beloved friends there growing in grace and a meetness for heaven. Their kindness and hospitality are really oppressive. My dear aunt is very feeble. She told me she enjoyed a heaven upon earth when in her room reading her Bible and praying. 'O the precious promises!' she exclaimed. 'Yes, "the blood of Jesus Christ cleanseth from all sin;" and, glory be to God! *I feel it.*'

"*October 7th.*—When committing my temporal concerns to God, I have felt more drawn to pray for entire resignation to His will, and power to glorify Him in every situation and circumstance than to ask for prosperity and enlargement of our borders. . . . I trust I can say,—

'And more I joy to gain Thy grace
Than all earth's treasures can afford.'

I covet not worldly riches, but I strive to economise in everything, and desire to be able to 'provide things honest in the sight of all men.'

"*December* 23rd.—Of late I have been permitted to feel a degree of holy joy. At times my cup has been full and running over. 'Bless the Lord, O my soul; and all that is within me, bless His holy Name!' All the young ladies have sought and found 'peace with God through our Lord Jesus Christ.'

"*January* 13th, 1828.—I am spared to see another year; and, what is best of all, to feel an increasing desire after holiness and more of every grace of the Holy Spirit. My soul is happy, and I have a firm confidence in God.

"*February* 3rd.—O for a more intense hungering and thirsting after righteousness! I want to love God with all my heart, and to feel a constant sense of His presence and approbation. Good old Mrs. Shapter enjoys this. Her conversation quickens and animates my soul. On Friday she said to me, 'O my dear Mrs. Shaw, praise the Lord on my account! I bless Him, I feel I am saved. It might discourage some, and cause others to despise religion, to make a profession of holiness; but I feel its reality.' *I* find the best way is to come this moment, and with a loving, humble, grateful, believing heart plead the promises and rely on my Saviour, Who sends none empty away.

"*March 8th.*—Called on Rev. — Chilcott, who conversed very freely on experimental religion. I left the Missionary Report with him. He told me that when he was twelve years old he was examined in Latin and Greek by that great and good man, the Rev. John Wesley, at Kingswood. He recollected the time with pleasure and should never forget it.

"*July* 20*th.*—On Thursday, June 19th, I was favoured, for the *first* time, with seeing all my seven children together; and my feelings are not easily described when we went to chapel to present ourselves before the Lord in His house. May parents and children finally meet at the right hand of God to praise the riches of redeeming grace!

"*December* 28*th.*—At present I am very

unwell, and thoughts of eternity impress my mind. I feel a weaning and loosening of my affections from all terrestrial things. I wish to live in the will of God.

"*March 8th*, 1829.—I have for years felt much pleasure in the distribution of religious tracts. Within the last few weeks we have endeavoured to establish a Tract Society. I have lent or given some hundreds of tracts to begin with, and I trust this plan will be attended with good. So many objects of distress have been discovered by the visitors, that a benevolent society seems an indispensable accompaniment. The scenes of misery and tales of woe have deeply affected my mind, and called forth sympathy and effort to afford relief as far as prudence would permit. Not being able to do as I would, I applied to a benevolent lady, who sent £5 to the clergyman for the poor of the parish. This sum was laid out in blankets; but the distribution was, of course, very limited, and bigotry prevailed so far that some of the needy applicants were told they were only to be given to true Church people!

"*April 5th*, 1830.—I am surrounded with

innumerable mercies, and feel it is not the least that so many of my children have their faces Zionward.

"*April* 19*th.*—The anniversary of my birthday. Fifty-seven years old! A time of profitable reflection. I took tea at Mr. T.'s. The visitors were Methodists. The members of the family, except one daughter, were not. I sought to give the conversation a profitable turn, and suggested to some present, 'Cannot we have singing and prayer?' I was entreated not to mention it. Mr. T., it was said, would by no means consent and might violently oppose. However, seeing, as I thought, a favourable opportunity, I rose to take leave, and taking Mr. T. by the hand I said, 'It is our practice, as Methodists, when we meet together to have singing and prayer before we part; but we are in your house, and I do not know if it will be agreeable. If you have no objection, it will make our visit more profitable.' 'O,' he replied, 'I have no objection if you wish it!' Mr. W. T. gave out a hymn and prayed, after which our host expressed his approbation, and I returned home thankful that I had been enabled to take up the cross. Lord

Jesus, let me ever feel Thee to be my Wisdom and Counsellor!

June 22nd.—Mr. Samuel Entwisle died almost suddenly. While his brother stepped into an adjoining room to get some fruit, he was seized with the cough, and ruptured a blood-vessel. Before his parents could arrive he was expiring, happy in God. He was one of the most exemplary young men I ever heard of. His father says he never had occasion to correct or even to reprove him from his infancy.

" *July 1st.*—After preaching, met in the public bands.

" *September 26th.*—O how many are the briers and thorns we meet with in the wilderness! How difficult and yet how necessary it is to keep the eye single, and to watch in all things, and to follow Jesus! The disorderly and immoral conduct of some of our old members during the excitement of the election has much grieved me. Alas! for Methodism when Bible precepts are set aside as useless.

" *May 29th.*—Being detained at a village for some hours waiting for a conveyance, I embraced the opportunity of calling at the different cottages with tracts, and saying something to the poor inmates respecting their everlasting concerns. In such employment I feel much pleasure. May Almighty God grant His blessing on the seed sown!

"*July* 24*th.*—On the coach I had a long conversation with a young gentleman, quite a man of fashion. He acknowledged that he had not studied the nature or the evidences of religion. O Thou Light and Life of the world, shine into his dark mind! And may I never be ashamed of Thee or of Thy truth!

"*December* 18*th.*—A very important event —the giving up my school, as I suppose, finally—took place on Thursday last. I have done with school! There is gratitude for past mercies, for having been providentially led into this arduous employment, and for having found pleasure in duty, and strength according to my day. Now that all my family are scattered, and my memory and strength are failing, my path seems to open clearly before me, and I hope to be led into a quiet resting-place."

Thus gratefully does Mrs. Shaw mention her retirement from school work, after having been engaged in it for ten years. At times her difficulties had been great; and from the day on which her school was opened until the day she left it, she felt her responsibility to be exceedingly heavy, but with thorough consistency and unflagging zeal she aimed at the intellectual and spiritual advancement of her pupils, and to a pleasing degree her efforts proved successful. God often leads His people by a way that they know not. Mrs. Shaw was induced somewhat reluctantly to engage in tuition, but she never had cause to regret the step. On the contrary, I believe she was always ready, as in the foregoing entry, to thank God for it. Perhaps no part of her useful life was more fruitful in blessed results than the years she spent at Buckfastleigh.

No one can read the manuscripts of our friend, written during these ten years, without noting her deep concern in reference to her children. Their temporal interests were not overlooked, but she was specially anxious to see them all walking in the truth. Great indeed was her joy when she beheld them, without an exception, members of the Church, and, as she had reason to believe, going with her heavenward.

She loved her children wisely, and sought to make home happy.

CHAPTER X.

LIVING TO PURPOSE.

ON leaving Buckfastleigh, Mrs. Shaw removed to St. Austell, and took up her abode with her afflicted brother, Mr. Joseph Flamank. Here she was blessed with many comforts, and surrounded by many friends. While home duties claimed her attention and were not neglected, she took an active interest in church-work and philanthropic effort, and found more than enough to occupy her thoughts and hours. But even now she was not exempt from sorrow. To have been entirely freed from that, she must have gone out of the world altogether.

It was her lot to mourn over the decease of three of her beloved children. With a loving mother's care she had watched over them in their early days, trained them "in the nurture and admonition of the Lord," and rejoiced over them when they made the start for heaven. She had followed them to their own homes with her blessings and her prayers. She had congratulated and counselled them when parental duties devolved on them. Indeed she had done all that a mother could do, and the hope was entertained by her that by-and-by they would lay her bones to rest. But in the mysterious arrangement of the Great Father, she who gave them birth had also, Rachel-like, to weep at their grave.

The first to pass away was her son Edmund, a man of exemplary character and a scholar of profound and varied attainments. His mother could say of him as a child that she never knew him tell an untruth, or disobey his parents. He gave his heart to God when yet a youth, and remained a consistent member of the Methodist Society till his death, which took place in 1833. The journal contains a touching account of his last illness, the struggle, and the victory. "O how can I describe the final scene!" wrote the troubled one. "My heart was too big to utter a word, but these lines came to my remembrance,—

'Angels now are hovering o'er us,
    Unperceived they join the throng.'

As he breathed his last my prayer was
'Lord Jesus, receive his spirit.'   Doubtless
he is now among the blood-washed company
before the throne."

Papers now lying before me furnish ample
evidence that Mr. Edmund Shaw's literary
attainments were of a high order.   As a
youth he was studious beyond his years;
and he so distinguished himself as a pupil
at Kingswood School that the late Mr. W. G.
Horner of Bath—assuredly no mean autho-
rity—refers to him as the Coryphæus of all
whom he remembered to have examined.
His subsequent career as a student was
eminently successful.   He had early made
great proficiency in Mathematics and Natural Philosophy.   He was critically acquainted
with the Greek and Latin languages, which
he wrote both in prose and verse with a spirit
and grace not common even at our Uni-
versities.   He was well versed in English
literature and familiar with French and
Italian; and his reading in the various

branches of Mental and Moral Philosophy was extensive and profound. He was, indeed, to quote the words of the Rev. John Lomas, who knew him intimately, " singularly gifted and highly cultivated." His teaching as Head Master of Kingswood School, is remembered with gratitude by many now living. Resigning this post on his marriage in 1829, he opened a school in Bath, where his career of usefulness was prematurely closed by his death, which was widely lamented, in the thirtieth year of his age.

" St. Austell, *September 2nd*, 1832.—Many have been recently called away by that desolating scourge—the cholera. Dr. Clarke finished his course on Sunday night last, and to-day our pulpit is hung in black. I felt much on hearing of his death. Forty-seven years ago last January I received my note of admittance into the Methodist Society from him. Ah, how slow has been my progress heavenward! Yet, blessed be God! I am pursuing, and trust I shall finally attain the goal.

" *November 4th.*—I have been requested to

form a new Female Class. On Tuesday week
only one person came. On Tuesday last six
came. I feel it to be a very important
charge. Lord Jesus, fully qualify me to
direct and lead these precious souls to
Thee!

"*March* 11*th*, 1833.—I have a hope through
the merits and intercession of the Lord
Jesus that I shall soon be with Him to
behold His glory, to contemplate His infinite
perfections, and perhaps to be employed in
some glorious work of which at present I
can form no just conception. O to be fully
prepared for the coming of my Lord!

" *April* 7*th.* — To-day Mr. M'Donald
preached a funeral sermon for Mr. Samuel
Drew, to the most crowded congregation
I ever saw, from Psalm lxxiii. 24—26. In
the loss of tried and dear friends I feel
differently from what I formerly did. My
mind is solemnly impressed at the change
they have experienced; but the thought that
I shall soon follow seems calculated to stir
me up to greater diligence that I may be
found ready.

" *October* 13*th.*—Of late God has been

pleased to discover to me some of the evils of my nature, especially pride, and the sight has so deeply affected me and caused such self-abasement that I have been constrained to say,—' I am all unclean, unclean ; Thy purity I want.' I am thankful for the discovery, as it does not drive me to despair, but to adore the all-sufficiency of the Saviour ' to cleanse from all unrighteousness.'

" *November* 10*th.*—I have derived much spiritual benefit from reading the Memoirs of my excellent and highly esteemed friend, the late Rev. William Lavers, who finished his course at Honiton two years ago. He was truly ' a burning and a shining light,' and enjoyed in a high degree the sanctifying influences of the Holy Spirit. I would not only admire but imitate.

" *January* 5*th*, 1834.—I praise my God that the fear of death is removed, and that I feel that He is love. I pray for an increase of faith and devotedness to God, and to be led into all truth doctrinal, practical and experimental. I find now, as I never did before, not only resignation, under my late painful bereavement—the loss of my excellent son

Edmund—but a disposition to praise God for having taken him from this state of trial to one of endless felicity.

"*February* 23rd.—After our last Bible-meeting the president stayed behind the rest, and we had much conversation on experimental religion. She is a most amiable woman, and a lady of high position, but wants clearer views and more feeling as to the necessity of the new birth unto righteousness. This heart-felt religion is the only thing needed to make her all that is lovely and excellent. I felt freedom in speaking to her, and often do I pray that she may be led into the way of peace and truth."

Thus did Mrs. Shaw "sow beside all waters." Her words were addressed to the rich as well as to the poor. In her opinion it was neither desirable nor right that the poverty-stricken should have *all* the attention of the Church, and that amongst these exclusively Mission-work should be carried on. To some of the wealthy it was Mrs. Shaw's pleasure to convey the message of mercy; and in cases not a few she had the joy of knowing that that message was received with thankfulness.

The following letters were addressed to a lady of title :—

" MY DEAR MADAM,—

" I beg you will receive my thanks for your kind remembrance in sending the short memoir of good old P. E. I cannot doubt her testimony to the truth and faithfulness of God which afforded her such strong consolation in the hour of trial. Though the doctrines of the forgiveness of sins, the Spirit of adoption, and assurance, are doubted by some, and denied by others, yet the Christian who desires to be taught of God, and to know His will, and who prayerfully searches the Bible will find in that blessed Book those doctrines clearly and fully set forth as the privilege of the children of God. . . . As our Almighty Creator is a God of love and designs our happiness, He most graciously and condescendingly points out to us the way of life, and invites us to come unto Him, with a promise that He ' will in no wise ' cast us out.

" In making these few free remarks to you, my dear Madam, I wish to assure you of the great respect and high esteem I feel for you in your exalted station, and to express my best wishes for your happiness here, and for your eternal felicity. Yet as children of fallen Adam, and beings that must exist for ever, we stand on common ground. For the prince and the beggar there is only one Bible, one Saviour, one Heaven.

" That we may be 'led into all truth,' enjoy the fulness of Gospel privileges and be the happy partakers of 'the Spirit of adoption,' retaining it with 'the full assurance of hope unto the end,' is the earnest prayer of

" My dear Madam,

" Yours most respectfully and affectionately,

" E. S."

" MY DEAR MADAM,—

" As I believe you regard me as a friend who sincerely wishes your happiness, and would rejoice in your spiritual prosperity, I cannot but deeply lament that anything should occur to prevent your enjoyment of those blessings which a wise and gracious God so freely offers as the purchase of His Son's blood. Life at all times is uncertain, and I regard myself as standing on the verge of the eternal world, having soon to give an account of my stewardship. . . . Allow me, therefore, my dear Madam, to address you with all the freedom of friendship, and as in the presence of Him Who will shortly be our Judge.

"In setting out on our Christian course it is needful to reflect and count the cost. The Bible affords ample information. We are told that 'all who will live godly in Christ Jesus shall suffer persecution.' If the world hate you, ye know that it hated Me before it hated you,' said the Saviour. 'Wherefore come out from among them, and be ye separate, saith the Lord, and touch not the unclean thing.' These with many other passages of like import teach us that while 'wide is the gate, and broad is the way that leadeth to destruction, and many there be which go in thereat,' still 'narrow is the way, that leadeth unto life.' This is our state of trial; the *next* that of rewards and punishments. Is it not then our highest wisdom to be imitators of Him ' Who for the joy that was set before Him endured the cross, despising the shame'? What can possibly bear comparison with the value of the immortal soul? or who can describe the folly and infatuation of him who runs the fearful risk of being doomed to endless perdition for the sake of obtaining the applause or avoiding the censure of his fellow-mortals? 'Know ye not,' says St. James, ' that the friendship of the world is enmity with God? Whosoever therefore will be a friend of the world is the enemy of God.'

"I am well aware, my dear Madam, that you are peculiarly circumstanced. Your situation requires great decision of character. You need much firmness, much of the Divine presence, and a lively persuasion of the realities of the invisible world and the Judgment day. . . . O that I could hope that anything I may be permitted to suggest might so influence your mind as to cause you to resolve from this time that you will

be a follower of the despised Saviour Who
was 'a Man of sorrows, and acquainted with
grief'! I believe that if you were decided
to devote yourself to God, though you might
for a time be exposed to opposition, perhaps
to scorn, contempt and ridicule, yet ultimately you would live down opposition and
have the happiness of seeing the influence
of your pious example in the conversion of
those who are dearest to you. O, my dear
Madam, be

> 'Bold to take up, firm to sustain
> The consecrated cross'!

"For your encouragement think of the
honour conferred on those among the ancient
worthies who had 'trial of cruel mockings
and scourgings, yea, moreover, of bonds and
imprisonment.' Be an imitator of those
who 'through faith and patience inherit the
promises.' ... For some time past I have
been led to pray with increased ardour in
your behalf that the many amiable qualities
you possess may be all turned into the right
channel, and flow from supreme love to
God. ... Perhaps this may be the last
faithful warning I may be permitted to

address to you. May God in much mercy bless the feeble though well-meant effort!

"That all the purchased blessings of Christ may richly descend on you in time and for ever is the earnest prayer of

"Your very affectionate and sincere friend,

"E. S."

"*August* 1*st*, 1834.—This morning—an ever-memorable one for the poor negroes—I rose early and went to the prayer-meeting in the Baptist chapel. Many prayed excellently, and my feelings were indescribable. I know not if ever I felt such melting, grateful adoration. I was indeed happy beyond expression. O may the liberated Africans be made free indeed, and glorify God with all their ransomed powers!

"*December* 21*st*.—My strength 'faileth; but God is the strength of my heart, and my portion for ever.' . . . I have been much pleased and profited in reading Mr. Watson's Life.

"*January* 18*th*, 1835.—On viewing a worm through a microscope its beauties appeared so dazzling as to be indescribable.

They most nearly resembled silver, glass, diamonds and the colours of the rainbow. . . . This little circumstance led to various thoughts of heaven and the employments there. Surely there is nothing irrational in the thought that the beauties of creation will be one of the subjects to delight those redeemed, bright intelligences who surround the throne of God! There there will be no need of the help of glasses to assist our vision in beholding His wonderful works.

"*April* 19*th.*—I am spared to see another return of my birthday, having been sixty-two years in the world. O for increasing gratitude to the Great Author of my life, and the Giver of every good and perfect gift!

"*February* 7*th,* 1836. — Dr. Bunting's excellent sermon from 'O Israel, thou shalt not be forgotten of Me,' (preached at St. Austell on the 27th ult.?) has proved very encouraging. I hear that his sermon at St. Ives on 'Seek ye first the kingdom of God, and His righteousness, etc.,' was made a peculiar blessing. This evening, while engaged in secret prayer before going to chapel, I was blessed with a most gracious manifestation of Divine love. Truly the intercourse was open between God and my soul!"

It will afford pleasure to every reader to peruse a well-written sketch of Mrs. Shaw from the eloquent pen of the Rev. Samuel W. Christophers. As his reminiscences of "the saintly woman" carry us back to this period of her life, I think it well to insert them here.

"I FIRST became acquainted with Mrs. Shaw in the summer of 1835. The privilege of an introduction to her just then appears to me to be one of those blessings of a kind Providence on which the stamp of Divine goodness is the deeper from their being so graciously timed. I had been sent to St. Austell to assist the Rev. Wilkinson Stephenson, whose health had failed. For a raw young man, as yet a ' babe in Christ,' and having but recently made his first effort to call his neighbours to repentance, to be suddenly called out of business into such a position was rather a severe trial, especially as Mr.

Stephenson bore so high a reputation, while the leading members of the St. Austell congregation, at that time, were far above the common standard of mental power, intellectual attainments and religious influence.

"There was at first some difficulty about my residence, and in the emergency Mrs. Shaw, with motherly kindness, received me into her house. Thus I was brought into daily intercourse with one whose manners, conversation, spirit and example, yea, whose very presence, had a happy and holy influence on my character and pursuits through life. At our first meeting her appearance seemed pleasantly to restore all the better associations of my childhood. The plain garb of the leading Methodist women, whose forms used to move around me in early life, was that worn by Mrs. Shaw. However peculiar it might seem to those who followed other modes, nothing could be more becoming and graceful than Mrs. Shaw's neat simplicity of dress. While I looked at her I seemed to be brought into living connection with the unworldly women of early Methodism. From the first I felt that in her presence I

was always in the presence of a lady. There
was a dignity of bearing so beautifully har-
monized with that meekness and quietness
of spirit 'which is in the sight of God of
great price,' that it seemed as if her motto
was an inspired passage which she once told
me had deeply impressed her while in secret
devotion, 'Thy gentleness hath made me
great.'

"Her spiritual-mindedness soon made
itself felt. Her spiritual discernment was
clear and keen. She was one of those 'who
are of full age,' those who 'by reason of use
have their senses exercised to discern both
good and evil.' The faithful tenderness
with which she watched over me, the vigi-
lant kindness with which my comfort was
promoted, the delicate attention to everything which, in my circumstances, could
render my work most easy and effective, will
never be forgotten. Indeed, they have never
ceased to influence my life for good. Mrs.
Shaw's character seems to me to have been
matured amidst sanctified trial. The foundation of her Christian character had been
laid during the life of Wesley, her know-

ledge of whom she liked to talk about, and whose influence and conversation had helped to give a decided and distinctive character to her piety. As a Christian she had realised her ' first love ' in companionship with some of the first Methodists. That ' first love ' was never lost. It continued to be the secret of that amiable consistency for which she was so remarkable. To me the consistency and fine balance of her character gave great weight to her counsels. She was wise in counsel; and advice from her lips still lives among the treasures of my heart. Those of my sermons which have been most fruitful to myself and to the people who have heard them were founded on texts which she recommended to my notice, as suggested to her during her private communion with God; and were thought out and first preached under the influence of her prayers. Her timely cautions, her faithful estimates of my spiritual and mental life and action, her judicious administration of encouragement and restraint were such as might dispose one to believe that she had deeply drunk into the spirit of those who so happily ruled the counsels and directed the movements of early Methodism. There was the same un-worldliness, simplicity, purity, quiet power, order and singleness of heart and aim. My life has been unspeakably the better for a lengthened enjoyment of her friendship. My soul holds her memory very dear. She was revered and loved by all who knew her as ' a mother in Israel,' but verily she was ' a mother in Israel ' to me."

CHAPTER XI.

"CONTINUANCE IN WELL-DOING."

In September, 1837, Mrs. Shaw paid a visit to her much-beloved son-in-law, the late Rev. Joseph Entwisle, then stationed in the Exeter Circuit. This visit she greatly enjoyed, and of the good influence of his prayers, conversation and public ministry she makes grateful mention in her diary. "Mr. Entwisle," she writes, "appears to be one of the most holy, heavenly-minded men I ever knew. He is altogether a Christian."

In 1839 she had to record the death of another of her children. Her son Thomas, who was in business at St. Ives, Cornwall, after a lingering illness, fell asleep in Jesus, and his sorrowing widow, worn out with grief and fatigue, after a few weeks, was laid to rest in the same grave. This double bereavement, while it wrung the mother's heart, also caused great anxiety, and entailed

on her frequent journeys and much correspondence. Still her peace was undisturbed :
she continued trusting in the Lord.

About two years after the death of Thomas,
her younger daughter, Mrs. Solomon, paid
a visit to her parents' house at St. Austell,
as it was hoped, to recruit her strength, but,
as it proved, to die.

It is not surprising, therefore, to find in
the journal mention of debility and prostra-
tion. Mrs. Shaw, in her love to her dear
suffering children, felt it to be her duty to
be as much as possible with them, to nurse
them with her own hand, and to cheer them
with her own voice, as well as to hear them
speak of their trust in the Lord Jesus Christ.
This consolation was hers, but the mental
and physical strain was very great. Indeed,
at one time there was such extreme weakness, attended with hemorrhage, that she
expected soon to be with those who had
already crossed the flood. She was brought
very low; but the Lord helped her and
raised her up again.

I copy a few extracts from her journal
written during these years of trial.

" *January 7th,* 1838.—This afternoon I attended a very solemn, profitable service. Many country friends were present. Mr. Hobson officiated. After the renewal of the Covenant, the Sacrament of the Lord's Supper was administered. I had looked forward with pleasing anticipation, hoping that the power of the Highest might overshadow us; and truly it was good to be there. I cannot say when I so fully enjoyed that blessed ordinance, or more sincerely dedicated my all to Him Who has purchased me with His own blood.

" *February 25th.*—I have received a letter from an old acquaintance, formerly in comparative affluence, but now in want. I feel much for him, and have made known his pitiable case to several friends. My hope is to be able to send him some relief.

" *August 19th.*—When thinking of my dear children, I feel the force of the remark, ' A mother lives in many lives.' I pray for entire submission to God's blessed will, strength according to our day, a sanctified use of every painful dispensation and a readiness to praise Him for His boundless mercies.

" *January* 13*th*, 1839.—Still kept by the
power of God through faith looking unto
Jesus. Yesterday Dr. Bunting called unex-
pectedly. He says the Meetings* have been
delightful: much piety, unity and liberality.
To God be all the glory!

" *February 3rd.*—I have recently attended
the Centenary Meeting at Truro. The President gave out the appropriate hymn,
' See how great a flame aspires,' and read
1 Chronicles xxix. Mr. Hobson engaged in
prayer. He was deeply affected, and the
whole congregation appeared much excited.
The President then gave a detailed account
of the rise and progress of Methodism, the
conversion of the two Wesleys, Peter Böh-
ler's blessed instrumentality, J. Nelson, etc.;
a most interesting account, which, though
long, I could have remained longer without
fatigue to hear. The Meeting lasted three
hours and a quarter."

In October, 1839, Mrs. Shaw undertook
a journey to Dover in charge of her little
grandchild, Thomas, and for the first time

* In connection with the Centenary of Methodism.

she travelled by rail ; thirty miles of the Great Western Railway being then open. In passing through London on her return, she only gave herself time to attend a Centenary Tea-meeting at City Road Chapel; and on the following day, leaving nearly all the London sights unseen, she hastened home. The seven hundred miles might easily and rapidly be traversed *now*, but it was not so easily done then ; and it is not surprising, therefore, that Mrs. Shaw should at some length describe the journey, and give God special thanks when brought back in peace.

" *February 9th*, 1840.—Last night I was led to ruminate on past events, and especially on my last interview with my beloved Thomas. Tears prevented my sleeping for a considerable time. To-day my spirits have been depressed. . . . I have felt reproved for speaking lightly of the abilities of one of our preachers. I trust I shall be more on my guard in future.

" *March 8th.*—Wrote a letter to Mrs. G—, in which I aimed at being plain, affectionate and faithful. Knowing that all human effort must be unavailing unless accompanied by the Holy Spirit's influence, I prayed for light, Divine instruction and the blessing of my Heavenly Father on the effort. Blessed be God for nearer access to Him than I have felt for some time!

" *April* 12*th.*—On Monday Lady G. S——took tea with me, and stayed till nine o'clock. She is a very amiable woman. I longed to be made useful to her. She appeared affectionate, thankful and humble, but afterwards I was exercised with self-reproach and fear lest I should have omitted to say what I ought."

The above entry and many others make it apparent that Mrs. Shaw saw the importance of pressing on individuals as she had opportunity the claims of her Saviour, and that she acted accordingly. She was far from thinking her whole duty accomplished when she had attended the means of grace, led her Classes and instructed the members of her own household. "One by one" she conversed with her friends and neighbours respecting the common salvation, and her

manner of setting before them " the truth
as it is in Jesus " was so happy, that it was
almost impossible for any person to feel
offended with her.   On one occasion, while
she was faithfully warning a gentleman
whom she knew, he impatiently exclaimed,
" Upon my word, Mrs. Shaw, I would not
hear this from any one but you." And then,
as if ashamed of his haste, he added in a
milder tone, " But I believe you are right
after all." That belief followed and troubled
him.   The impression made on his mind
was deepened by the Good Spirit, and after
a while he became a follower of Christ.

" Some time since," writes Mr. John
Shaw, " two pious commercial gentlemen
informed me that through my mother's
instrumentality they were brought to God
when they were apprentices."

As a Class-leader Mrs. Shaw was highly
esteemed.   When time and strength permitted, she visited absentees, and when a
visit could not be paid she used her facile
pen.   The following extracts from letters are
sufficient to indicate the deep interest she
took in their spiritual prosperity, as well as

the fidelity with which she discharged the
duties of her important office:—

"June 27th, 1836.

"My dear Madam,—

"Having lately been prevented from calling on you by absence and indisposition, I
take the liberty of addressing a few lines to
you. .... The responsibility of my office
makes me deeply concerned to promote the
best interests of those who are so intimately
connected with me in Christian communion.
You have generally expressed yourself as
having been benefited by the means of grace.
On this account I have the more sincerely
lamented your absence from them. From
long experience I know that our grand
adversary hates, and, by every means in his
power, strives to destroy the work of grace
in our hearts. He never fails to throw
obstacles in our way, and hindrances to our
attendance on those ordinances which are
calculated to enlighten and quicken our
souls. ... Be assured that whatever will
tend to your happiness or spiritual profit I
shall most sincerely rejoice to find you have

adopted. I have thought whether you would prefer meeting in another Class, and with another Leader. If so, I would by all means advise you to change. Do not, my dear Madam, suppose that I should be offended. No; far from it. God has in His infinite wisdom and goodness endued us with different gifts and talents, and if another should be more useful than I have been, I shall rejoice in your prosperity. I trust you will act as in the sight of God, and go where you can profit most; for your happiness and increasing devotedness to God will always afford me much pleasure. The members of my Classes are daily remembered at a throne of grace, and your case, with that of one who is deeply afflicted, has been specially kept in mind.

" With kindest regards, believe me to be,
" My dear Madam,
" Your sincerely affectionate,
" E. S."

" September 13th, 1841.
" MY DEAR MISS L.,—
" Family afflictions, combined with other

engagements, have, for a long time past, prevented me from calling on you as I otherwise should have done. Of late I have been much grieved at your frequent absence from Class. I find from my paper that you have not been present since the 6th of April. I feel it is my painful duty to warn you to beware of a backsliding heart. The Spirit of God may be so grieved by sins of omission as to take His everlasting flight. O my dear Miss L—, let me entreat you to rouse yourself from your lethargy, cry mightily unto God, and be determined never to suffer the world or temporal gain to have the ascendency in your affections! The Scriptures assure us that 'if any man love the world, the love of the Father is not in him.' I cannot think that if God and religion were the supreme objects of your delight, you could neglect those means of grace which, as a Methodist, you have professed to approve, and which are highly calculated to quicken and benefit the soul. If you are an invalid, the hour of three o'clock is favourable, and the season of the year such as admits of no excuse. If you find that you cannot conveniently go out on a week-day, there are several Sunday Classes in which you might meet with less interruption; and I would advise you by all means to go to one of them. Do not forsake the assembling with the people of God. Life is short and uncertain; and it behoves us to give all diligence to secure our everlasting salvation. 'Work while it is day: the night cometh, when no man can work.' That you may seek and obtain an increase of every grace of the Holy Spirit, live in the enjoyment of vital religion, and finally inherit eternal life, is the sincere desire of

" Your affectionate friend,

" E. S."

" *September* 28*th*, 1840.—This is the thirty-eighth anniversary of our wedding-day. The review of the past has excited gratitude in my breast and constrained me to say, 'Surely goodness and mercy' have followed me all my days! My severest trials have proved blessings in disguise. They have driven me to a throne of grace, made Christ more

M

precious, weaned me from the world and from created good, and caused me to take firmer hold on heaven.

" *October* 18*th.*—I was glad to find that at our District Meeting it was decided to appoint this day as a day of thanksgiving to Almighty God for the abundant harvest. . . . I have of late been more than usually engaged in public affairs. . . . May I do all to please God, and be useful to my fellow-creatures. I desire to use every talent, whether of nature, providence or grace, to God's glory. . . . I feel great pleasure in relieving the wants of the poor, and pray that they may be fed with the Bread of Life.

" *November* 24*th.*—I have received the heart-cheering news that my dear Samuel has obtained a sense of the pardoning mercy and love of God. My heart overflows with gratitude, love and praise; and this verse has been uppermost in my mind all day :—

' My Saviour, how shall I proclaim,
    How pay, the mighty debt I owe ?
Let all I have, and all I am,
    Ceaseless to all Thy glory show.'

" *March* 24*th*, 1841.—Our Quarterly Meeting. God has graciously poured out His Spirit on the Circuit, so that between three and four hundred persons have received notes of admission, and give satisfactory accounts of the work of grace in their hearts.

" *September 5th,* 1841.—On August 9th my dear Libby [Mrs. Solomon] escaped to the haven of eternal repose, and left us to follow. O the pangs I felt in the awful moment of separation! The week before she died she was enabled to say, 'O death, where is thy sting? O grave, where is thy victory?... Thanks be to God, which giveth me the victory through our Lord Jesus Christ.'

" *November 22nd.*—This day, forty-two years since, my ever dear Robert Green exchanged mortality for eternal life.* O what a blessed change! May I be found ready whenever the Master calls!... On Friday, the 5th inst., I received a letter from my dear Harriet in which she named some presents which their dear Father Entwisle had made them, particularly a repeating watch which had

---

* Mr. Green died in November, 1799, *not* in January, 1800, as before stated by mistake.

formerly been the late Rev. J. Pawson's. A thought passed my mind that Mr. Entwisle seemed to be arranging all his affairs as though he had a presentiment of being soon removed to a better world. On the following Tuesday the post brought another letter from Tadcaster. On perusing it, to my astonishment I found that dear old Mr. Entwisle was called suddenly to his eternal reward on the 6th instant about ten o'clock. This awfully sudden bereavement has caused the friends to feel the painful separation most acutely; though to him it was almost a translation. Only a few minutes passed between his being as well as usual, and his entry into the mansions of light and glory; and so sweetly and insensibly did the change take place, that they scarcely knew when he ceased to breathe.

"*May* 1*st*, 1843.—I have now attained my threescore years and ten, and, blessed be God! I trust my soul is alive to Him, and earnestly desires a full meetness for that eternal inheritance which is promised to them that love Him.

" *May* 21*st*.—The state of public affairs appears to be deeply important and portentous. My private opinion, for many years, has been that we may be permitted to pass through a fiery ordeal of persecution for a season, that this will tend to purge the dross, purify the graces of real Christians, separate the precious from the vile and promote love and union among all the true disciples of Jesus, and that from this dark night the real Church of Christ will emerge as the sun from a cloud and shine with resplendent brightness. Truth will ultimately triumph, and Jesus will reign over all the earth. Let Thy Kingdom come, and prepare us for Thyself.

" *September* 3*rd*.—This evening I was led to contemplate the nearness of the eternal world, and had such a sense of my unfaithfulness, forgetfulness of God and innumerable shortcomings as I cannot well describe. I thought, ' What can I do? I nothing have, I nothing am.' Just then the view of the Atonement presented to my mind was such that I felt I could trust and not be afraid. O the blessings which flow from the cross

of Christ! What a short, certain and easy
way to *come*, resting on the atoning blood;
to feel that Jesus has loved *me*, and given
Himself for *me;* that He is mine, and I am
His! Never before did I so fully see the
force of the words—

'Other refuge have I none,
Hangs my helpless soul on Thee.'

" *November* 6th.—Last evening I received
the solemn and sorrowful tidings of my
dear sister Fanny Colenso's death. I was
deeply affected. My dear little Emily, not
yet six years old, after for a time sitting
quite silent, while tears of sympathy ran
down her cheeks, came and kissed me, saying, ' Don't grieve, my dear Grandmamma,
I will read you a chapter that will comfort
you.' She selected 1 Thessalonians v., and
having read that, she read chapter iv., and
noticed particularly from the 13th verse.

" *November* 12th.—Yesterday Emily told
me she was very sorry to see me so poorly.
I replied that God saw it best, and that He
could remove the sickness; but that He
could not err. She answered, ' I know it is

said in the Bible " Whom the Lord loveth
He chasteneth,"' and then added, ' O, I
should like to see my dear papa and my
little sister! but more than all I should
like to go to heaven to see my dear mamma!
I hope when my dear mamma looks for me
she will find me among the good.'

" *February* 21st, 1844.—I have been re-
viewing the way in which the Lord has led
me from my infancy to the present hour.
Sometimes He has thwarted my purposes,
and opposed my plans and designs ; and my
will has been crossed, I know not why.
Yet *afterwards* I have discovered the goodness and mercy of my God in thus over-
ruling circumstances which would have
involved me in distress and perplexity. I
feel that all His ways are just and true :
my soul is absorbed in gratitude, love and
praise.

" *June 3rd* (after a journey).—O how
manifold are the mercies and favours bestowed on me! the kindness and sympathy
of friends, the supply of my temporal wants,
and, above all, the refreshing influences of
the Holy Spirit. Often is my mind im-

pressed with the thought that I may possibly
be called suddenly away to appear before a
God of spotless purity.   I long for clearer
manifestations of Divine love.

" *June* 30*th.*—At Class I referred to a
subject which I have not mentioned before,
namely—conformity to the fashions of the
world in dress.   Some had remarked that
' they wondered how Mrs. Shaw could tolerate
such things in her Class, as she herself was
so plain.'   I referred to this, and read extracts from our venerable Founder's works.
I said some things by way of advice, the
result of much prayer for the teaching of
the Holy Spirit, and requested that each
would bring the matter before God.

" *April* 27*th*, 1845.—On Sunday our Missionary Anniversary Services commenced.
On the day of the Meeting we had several
strangers, including the Deputation, our
preachers and their wives to dine, take tea
and sup with us.   Though I passed my
seventy-second birthday on the 19th, and
our old servant is very feeble, God graciously
helped me.

" *June* 10*th.*—To-day I parted with our

precious little Emily. She has been with us more than four years, and is a very affectionate, good child."

"Our precious little Emily," mentioned above, and in former entries, was daughter of Mrs. Solomon, whose death has been referred to, and is now the wife of the Rev. James W. Eacott. In compliance with my request, she has kindly favoured me with the following remembrances of her sainted grandmother :—

" I lived with my beloved grandmamma when a child for four years, and corresponded with her until a short time before her death.

" I well remember her in her neat attire, always spotless as to cleanliness, her face expressive of the holy calm that reigned within. She *looked* good; and, though I was a mere child, everything about her made me love goodness. She was a strict disciplinarian, and never spared chastisement when serious faults were committed, but she wisely discriminated between these and mere childish errors.

" The most hallowed recollections are the precious Sabbath evenings which I spent at home with her in the winters.   How sweetly she talked to me of the love of Jesus in dying for *me!* and how affectionately she urged me to give my young heart to Him ! She believed in the recognition of friends in heaven, and also seemed to think that the departed were allowed to watch the loved ones on earth ; for she often talked to me of my own sainted mother, and wished me to act as if she could see my conduct.   But specially she tried to make me realise the constant presence of God.   Prayer she taught me to look upon as a blessed privilege as well as duty ; and she took advantage of every little incident (even so trivial a thing as the illness of a favourite kitten) to encourage me to bring my troubles to God and seek His aid.   She was ever on the watch to sow the good seed in my heart. I remember well the look of tender entreaty she turned on me when a minister was speaking of an interesting case of very early piety he had met with.   I bless God for her early instructions.

"When I left her she followed me with her counsels and her prayers. At this time (1845) she had passed her threescore years and ten, but was still actively engaged in the service of God and His Church.

"Her strong faith in the Atonement, her habit of prayer, her humility and the warm interest which she took in the cause of God are strikingly apparent in her correspondence.

"In 1858 I had the pleasure and privilege of spending a month with her. During this visit, I made notes of some of her remarks, feeling them to be 'weighty words.' These are samples:—'Always act truly, honestly, faithfully.' 'Acknowledge God in all your ways, and He will direct your paths.' 'There is only one life worth living.' "

As the foregoing testimony shows, Mrs. Shaw's kindness to and sympathy with children and young persons were very great. She loved them fondly, but she was careful not to spoil them. Her manner was winsome. In her mode of address there was much of the attractive, nothing of the repel-

lent. Even in extreme old age she delighted
to speak of the claims of God and the
importance and blessedness of serving Him
throughout the whole of life. Two children
of the writer will not soon forget the kind
and cheery way in which she took each by
the hand, and quoted the wise man's counsel,
" Remember now thy Creator in the days of
thy youth."

The following extracts from letters addressed to Mrs. Eacott, afford further illus-
tration of this trait in Mrs. Shaw's character :—

" I quite long to hear from you how you
are and what you are doing. We miss you
very much, and many tears have I shed
since you left us because my affectionate
little Emily is gone. I hope, my dear,
that you try to be good, and seek to be
useful to your dear mamma and sisters.
Always remember that God sees you, and
knows all your thoughts and all your desires :
therefore study to please Him. Then you
will be happy, and prepared for His everlasting kingdom. Both your bird and cat

are well. ' Dicky ' is losing his feathers, and does not sing so sweetly as he used to do.

" *July* 1*st*, 1845.—As I am busy I have not time to say much to you; but I must thank you for your letter, and beg you to write again soon. Ever remember, my dear, that the way to insure true happiness is to ' love God and keep His commandments,' to be obedient to your dear parents, and affectionate and kind to all. Seek to be usefully, diligently and constantly employed. If you have nothing to do, Satan will set you to do mischief, and make you very miserable. Your bird, though moulting, is very well, and sang a sweet song this morning while we were at breakfast. Pussy is also well, but does not visit the parlour so often as when her kind friend Emily was here. Read my advice to you again and again: and if you love me as I love you, you will not forget

" Your very affectionate Grandmamma.

" *September* 12*th*, 1845.—Often, very often, do I think of you, and pray for you that you may by prayer and watchfulness, be

preserved from every improper temper, word
and action. Remember, my dear, that the
eye of God is always upon you. No secret
thought can be concealed from Him, and He
delights to hear your sincere prayers. He
will bless you if you ask Him and strive to
please Him in all things. I hope you will
be able to read this plain writing. Your
beautiful ' Dicky ' sings charmingly, and
pussy is well.

" *November 7th*, 1846.—I wish to assure
you that you are not forgotten by your
Grandmamma. I often think of you and
pray that the Holy Spirit may shine more
and more clearly into your heart, showing
you the great depravity of your nature and
the necessity of earnestly seeking grace to
resist every temptation to evil and power to
love and serve God continually. O my
dear Emily, be watchful and prayerful:
then you will be happy! God is love. He
delights to bless and save all who come unto
Him ; especially young disciples.

" *October 20th*, 1854.—Let me beseech you

never be ashamed to own the Master Whom you serve. . . . By steady perseverance you may be made a blessing to those around you. . . . I long to know that your dear sister is fully resolved to devote her heart, her life, her all to God. Present my best love to her, and tell her from me that *religion is the only thing that can make her happy*, and that now, *in my eighty-second year, I feel it to be increasingly precious.*

"*April* 23rd, 1857.—I thank you, my dear, for your kind congratulations on the attainment of my eighty-fourth birthday. No doubt your hopes were prompted by affectionate regard; but I could not join in the wish that either your dear Grandpapa, who attained his ninetieth year in January, or myself might see *many* returns of the day on earth. The infirmities of old age I *never* thought desirable. Now that we feel them, it behoves us to pray that we may live in the will of God, and be fully meet for His kingdom. . . . You ask me to give you my views respecting entire sanctifica-tion. I must refer you to Mr. Wesley's

' Christian Perfection.' He wrote clearly and to the point. Though there are many excellent treatises on the subject and many memoirs which are helpful, yet none ever so profited me as this work. I have found it to be invaluable."

Diary. "*September* 1*st*, 1845.—On July 3rd I gave up my office of Wardrobe Keeper for the Dorcas Society, which I have held for twelve or thirteen years; and on August 14th I gave up another office—that of Bible Secretary. I felt much about this, and shed a few tears; but was quite satisfied that at my age, with increasing infirmities, and having so many duties in my family, it was my duty to seek a successor. . . . Reading again Lady Maxwell's Life has been blessed to me. How have I desired to partake of her spirit, and to live in the exercise of prayer, devotion and sacrifice!

"*October* 26*th*.—When my beloved husband and I were in conversation on religious experience, I had such a proof of his kind, faithful and tender regard in affectionately reproving what he had observed contrary to

the Divine rule, as excited a more than
ordinary sense of grateful love and esteem.
' Faithful are the wounds of a friend.' I
perceive in him an increase of heavenly-
mindedness and deadness to the world.

" *November* 2*nd.*—I have been incessantly
engaged in public and domestic duties. We
have been collecting funds for the purpose
of furnishing the preachers' houses. It is
painful to meet with narrow-minded, covetous
persons, who give grudgingly. Were it in
my power I would much rather *give* than
ask for the trifles which they cannot with
any feeling of propriety withhold. Many
kindly bring a willing offering, and as
' God loveth a cheerful giver,' they will be
rewarded.

"*August* 24*th,* 1846.—On Monday, August
3rd, went to Bristol. I was rather too late to
hear the Ex-President's sermon, but I peeped
in at the side door to see the preachers
assembled in Conference. After taking tea
with Messrs. Haswell and Entwisle at Mr.
Lomas's, we went to the chapel, which
we found completely filled, and hundreds
going away not able to get admittance.

N

Messrs. Keeling and Roebuck took me round to the vestry where the Committees meet. Through the kindness of several who assisted me to get up, I reached the platform, and when one of the senior ministers withdrew, I was invited by the President to take his place. Being unknown, except to some of the preachers, I felt less than I otherwise should have done. It was an interesting opportunity to hear the young men give an account of their conversion, call to the ministry, etc. My mind was solemnly impressed in reflecting on the removal to a better world of *every* individual who had composed the Conference *sixty* years before, when Mr. Wesley—who once took me with him on a journey from St. Austell to Redruth, and back through Wadebridge and Port Isaac, and was accustomed to call me his ' little Betsey '—permitted me to go for a short time to the front of the gallery in Broadmead chapel that I might see the preachers. This was in 1786. In returning through the vestry I had the pleasure of shaking hands with many of our excellent men;—M'Owan, M'Donald, Jackson, the

American and Irish Deputations, T. Farmer, Esq., and others.

Of the Conference of 1786, Mr. Wesley writes, " About eighty preachers attended. We met every day at six and nine in the morning, and at two in the afternoon. . . . On Thursday in the afternoon we permitted any of the Society to be present, and weighed what was said about separating from the Church," etc. At that time the Methodist Societies in Great Britain and Ireland counted 58,156 members. Now, sixty years later, the numbers had increased to 369,014. Though God had buried His workmen, He had carried on His work.

And, blessed be God, it is ours to rejoice that He Who sustained and led the " excellent men " of whom Mrs. Shaw makes mention in her journal, who have fallen asleep— is with His servants still.

" THE BEST OF ALL IS, GOD IS WITH US."

CHAPTER XII

"FRUIT IN OLD AGE."

ALTHOUGH Mrs. Shaw had not as yet completed her pilgrimage within a quarter of a century, she found the weaknesses of old age coming upon her. Still, as failing health permitted, she continued to work for God. Her interest in passing events was unabated, and her love for "whatsoever things are true, etc.," was even greater than it had been in her youthful days.

Many of the entries in the journal during the latter years of her life relate to private matters; but some portions of the record, not of this description, are too valuable to be omitted. Those who have been sufficiently interested to read thus far, will find pleasure and profit in the perusal of the following extracts :—

"*April* 18*th*, 1847.—I feel pain, weakness and the infirmities of age, as may be expected. Should I live till to-morrow, it will be the seventy-fourth anniversary of my birthday. O what a life of mercies! God has been very gracious. He has dealt bountifully with me, and my chief desire is to be wholly His.

"*June* 13*th.*—On Friday a riot was occasioned by the advance in the price of flour. The clay-men assembled in great numbers. A party of soldiers was sent for, by express, from Bodmin; and these, with a hundred and seventy special constables, the sheriff, magistrates and principal gentlemen of the town, paraded the streets, and endeavoured, with great patience, to conciliate the infuriated mob. One man struck the sheriff, and the riot act was read, but no further acts of violence were committed. Fourteen of the rioters were taken into custody, and removed to Bodmin. The market was closed, shops shut, business suspended, and general consternation prevailed. Though sometimes such things affect me much, through mercy my mind was kept in peace. O that amid the scenes of this mortal life, I may be found watching and growing in grace!

"*July* 4*th*.—'Thus far on life's perplexing path' hath the Lord helped me, and comforted me. My mind is kept in a peaceful state, and I feel increased desires to obtain a full meetness for my heavenly inheritance, so that when the Master calls I may be found ready.

"*December* 12*th*.—I have found it profitable during the last few Sunday evenings to read over what I have written for my own benefit, and to call to remembrance the manifold mercies received, the supporting grace granted, the deliverances wrought out for me, and the many answers to prayer vouchsafed during the last ten years. I feel greater longings after holiness. . . . Our Class-meetings have been blessed seasons of 'refreshing . . . from the presence of the Lord.'

"*February* 20*th*, 1848.—Blessed be God for His great goodness and infinite condescension in stooping so low as to lend an ear to my supplications. I trust I have lately felt some increase of spiritual life, light and love. To-day I have enjoyed much communion with God, a sinking into

His will and gratitude for His providential care and the supply of all my needs ; without desiring more than He has given. I wish to be guided by Him in the distribution of what we have to spare. I do not think of laying up treasure on earth. If, by prudent economy and self-denial, I can save something from our annual income, it is that I may give.

"*March 26th.*—This day sixteen years ago we came to reside at St. Austell with my brother. . . . Since then what changes have taken place in our family! What bereavements, afflictions, chastenings, support and consolations have I experienced! Surely I may exclaim, ' His mercy endureth for ever' !

"*July 9th.*—O God, Thou Who art witness to the secret and sincere desires of my heart, Thou knowest that my whole dependence is on the Atonement and Intercession of my Lord and Saviour, and that I desire above all things to be such as Thou wilt approve! And though I lament my shortcomings, unfaithfulness and forgetfulness of Thee, yet I *do* love Thee, and would praise Thee for the innumerable blessings Thou hast bestowed and for Thy ' exceeding great and precious promises.' O Lord, increase my faith !

" *October* 4*th.*—I have been favoured, by the Rev. Joseph Entwisle, with part of his late father's memoirs. As far as I have read, the perusal has been very interesting and profitable. I have been led to self-examination, and feel earnest desires to copy his bright example.

"*November* 19*th.*—This morning I received from my dear son-in-law the engraving of his father's portrait—a most exact likeness.

"*December* 17*th.*—I have just received the account of dear Robert Rogers's * peaceful death. After having spoken most sweetly to his sister, as she held his hand in hers, he ceased to breathe, and his happy spirit entered into rest. I deeply sympathize with the family : their loss is great ; but *he* has reached the abode of eternal bliss. Age and

---

* Mrs. Shaw's nephew, son of the Rev. Thomas Rogers.

experience of the world cause Christians to view the departure hence in a different light from that in which they viewed it in younger days. The light of eternity dawns when seventy-five years have passed away. The aged one sees that the end desired—eternal glory—is obtained, and that it is the survivor's privilege, through faith in the Lord Jesus Christ, to say 'Thy will be done.' 'Thanks be to God, which giveth us the victory through our Lord Jesus Christ.'

"*January* 14*th*, 1849.—The beginning of a new year has been a season of renewed desires and purposes to live to and for God.

" *Good Friday, April* 6*th.*—I have been profited in reading the Memoirs of William Dawson and William E. Miller. God has mercifully showed me many evils that remain unsubdued. I pray for power and grace and faith in the blood of the Cross that these may be subdued, and that love, peace, humility and a constant cleaving to Jesus may be my portion. I have written letters to two friends, between whom a misunderstanding has arisen, and trust that as the result prejudice will be removed and peace restored.

"*August* 12*th.*—The cholera has visited Mevagissey, and its ravages have been most appalling. Many of the inhabitants have left the town. . . . O that this awful visitation may be overruled for good, and that the people may learn righteousness!

" *September* 19*th.*—This day has been set apart for humiliation and prayer on account of the cholera. In the morning we went to the church, and heard a useful and impressive discourse from Mr. Todd. Prayer-meeting at three o'clock in the Baptist chapel, and preaching, with many prayers, at half-past six in our own chapel. The shops have been closed, labour suspended and all the services well attended. May God hear prayer and say to the destroying angel, ' It is enough : stay now thine hand !' And may many turn unto the Lord.

" *November* 25*th.*—I have received a letter from Southampton in answer to mine of the 15th ult. in which I inquired about ten or a dozen old friends whom I had known, and I find that not one of them is now living !

"*April* 19*th*, 1850.—This is the seventy-seventh anniversary of my birthday. . . . Blessed be God I feel that I am His, and that He will do what is best with, and for me! I am surrounded with mercies.

"*June* 9*th*.—Deeply interested in reading Mrs. Elizabeth Fry's Life. What a life of useful, active, persevering effort in the cause of humanity, truth and righteousness was hers! Surely she will shine as a bright star for ever and ever!

"*September* 1*st*.—All thanks be ascribed to my Heavenly Father for innumerable blessings! My soul is in a more devotional, prosperous state than for a long time past. The article in the Magazine on 'Entire Sanctification' has been remarkably blessed to me in quickening and encouraging me to seek more earnestly for this privilege.

"*September* 29*th*.—On Thursday week I was requested to visit a young lady who was very ill and would not consent to see any religious person except myself. I felt deeply concerned, and feared how I might find her, and whether I should be able to speak suitably, as I have generally very faint hopes of sick-bed repentances. I was told of her former gaiety, and reserve on religious subjects; but was pleased to find her communicative. Her advantages when in Scotland had been superior to those of many with regard to religion, and her views appeared to be correct. She complained of want of deep and constant concern about eternal things, and of lack of fervour in prayer; feared she did not hate sin, and that if she were to recover she should still love the vanities of life. I spoke as plainly and affectionately as I could, prayed with her, and left believing her to be in a hopeful state. I saw her again on Saturday. Her voice was so low that I could not understand her, and her pain was so agonizing that she could not attend to prayer when it was proposed. On Monday I found her much better, able to converse freely and cheerfully. She said she loved God, was quite willing to suffer, felt no murmuring spirit, but gratitude for the many mercies she enjoyed, had no fear of hell, but a joyful expectation of heaven, and would rather die than live. After prayer I took leave, saying that I hoped to see her again on Wednesday, but that same afternoon her spirit took its flight. Most peaceful was her end, and a smile remained on her countenance. Her state was not altogether so satisfactory as I could have wished, although from her replies to my pointed questions, I cannot doubt but she is with the Lord.

" *October* 27*th.*—In nearness of access to God, entire submission to His blessed will and the spirit of praise and devotion last Sunday was one of the happiest days of my life. . . . My dear husband is very unwell. It appears to me as though this winter may be his last. In the anticipation of parting I feel much need of Divine support. He is very dear to me, and though God only knows who may be taken first,—for we are both failing and one cannot long survive the other,—yet I would, if put to the choice, prefer drinking the bitter cup myself, to leaving him behind to have to dwell among strangers. O Lord, fully prepare us for all Thy blessed will !

" *January* 4*th*, 1852.—Being permitted to see the beginning of another year, I wish

anew to devote myself to Him Who has
purchased me with His precious blood. On
Christmas-day I felt more than I ever
remember to have felt, the infinite love and
condescension of our adorable Saviour in
stooping so low as to assume our nature,
and suffer in our stead, that we might finally
attain everlasting life.

"*April* 25*th*.—I am astonished when I
think that I have entered on my eightieth
year. O how little fruit have I borne to
the glory of God! and yet I am spared, a
monument of the long-suffering of my com-
passionate Saviour."

CHAPTER XIII.

THE "MOTHER IN ISRAEL."

THOSE who live with us can speak the most confidently as to what we really are. I am thankful therefore to avail myself of the testimonies of those who dwelt in the same house with Mrs. Shaw, and had the most favourable opportunities of forming a correct judgment of her excellences and influence.

Mrs. Entwisle, widow of the late Rev. J. Entwisle, writes:—"In the government of her family my dear mother always endeavoured to combine firmness with kindness. We all knew full well that what mother *said*, mother meant; and that her instructions must be attended to, and that instantly. But such was the loving way in which she ruled that I believe it was the opinion of every one of us that no other children had such a good mother as we had. Then, as we grew up, our confidence in her was so great that we delighted to regard her as our best earthly friend, to whom we might confide every important step, and on whose opinion we might safely rely. In sound judgment respecting business matters few could surpass her. She was very careful in selecting her servants, and she usually kept them a long time,—eleven or twelve years when she became settled; and such good servants generally regarded her with child-like respect. She possessed a good share of quiet energy, and all her domestic arrangements were so orderly and exact as to contribute materially to the comfort of the family and domestics. Our meals were punctual to the minute, and whether in her chests of drawers and cupboards upstairs, or in the cellars, which were under her own immediate care, I believe she could have put her hand on anything she wanted, even in the dark. The importance of order, I need not say, she strongly inculcated on all of us, as one means of economizing both time and money."

Mr. John Shaw writes:—"I shall have abundant cause to praise God to all eternity for pious parents, and especially for an eminently pious mother. Connected with my earliest recollections are her tender love and the deep interest she took in our temporal welfare. But she evinced the most affectionate and earnest solicitude for our early conversion to God; and with the views propounded on this subject by the late Rev. Samuel Jackson she expressed the warmest sympathy. So far from discouraging, as many parents do, early conviction of sin, and the tearful concern shown by young children to love Christ, she believed that 'out of the mouth of babes and sucklings' His praises are 'perfected,' and she had the high joy of witnessing that her children, while yet young, remembered the Lord God of their parents. All became members of the Christian Church. Several preceded her to the heavenly kingdom, and her three surviving children are walking in the paths of godliness. When about eight years of age, one Sabbath evening, while listening to a sermon on the parable of 'the Barren

O

Fig-tree,' I felt that I resembled the un-
productive tree. I was convinced of my
guilty fruitlessness, and this affected me to
tears. My dear mother saw my concern,
and when we reached home she took me
into her room, and never shall I forget the
loving and earnest way in which she put her
hand upon my shoulder, and said, 'Now,
my dear John, while the Holy Spirit is thus
graciously striving, say,—

> 'Nay, but I yield, I yield ;
> I can hold out no more :
> I sink, by dying love compell'd,
> And own Thee Conqueror." '

Although I did not then become fully decided
for God, the impression made upon my mind
by the sermon and her counsels and prayers
ever after exerted a very salutary influence
upon my mind. When about fourteen years
of age I was again awakened to earnest
concern for my soul's salvation; and overcoming my natural backwardness and timidity in opening my mind to my parents on
religious subjects, I now frankly told them
of my sincere penitence and fear of the wrath
to come, and begged them to pray with and

for me.   This they gladly did, and their importunate and believing intercessions were answered in my happy conversion to God and union with the Church of Christ."

These testimonies are corroborated by the statements of those who, though they did not live with Mrs. Shaw, enjoyed her friendship for many years and often visited her. They watched her deportment during sunshine and storm, and their estimate of her excellences is not at all below that which has just been read.   It is satisfactory to be able to place before the reader the opinion of one who, though feeling something of the weight of fourscore years pressing upon him, still delights to labour in the Lord's service.   The venerable Mr. Stapleton of Tavistock, writes:—" I knew Mrs. Shaw intimately for forty-eight years.   I knew her as a friend, and as a Christian.   I knew her in the various relations of life, as mistress, mother and wife; and I may say that in all these respects I never met with her equal.   She was a pattern in neatness and order—prompt and decided, without

being intrusive or dogmatical. She was a
Methodist of the primitive stamp. Her
piety was deep and uniform—cheerful without levity, sedate without gloom. She was
' full of good works and alms-deeds,' and to
assist others she denied herself, in dress and
in other respects, of many things which she
even needed. She always carried her Bible
and note-book about with her. For some
years she was subject to palpitation of the
heart which at times threatened her with
instant death. On one occasion when walking alone, thinking the end had come, she
sat down by the road-side, took out her
pocket-book, and wrote in it the state of her
mind for the satisfaction of friends. From
her conversion she held on her way with
steady course; and tried, as a Christian, to
do and bear the will of God. Such was
her influence as a mother that all her
children were converted in early life, and
became members of the Methodist Society.
She had a clear, strong intellect, well cultivated, and brought under the wisdom from
above. Hence she was a wise counsellor:
her judgment might be depended on. When

I first knew her she had reached the noon
of her day, and was a vigorous, active, most
useful woman. As time passed on I watched
her course, and was honoured with her confidence. Her hold on God was firm. She
had deep, clear views of the atonement and
merits of Jesus; and generally enjoyed the
rich indwelling of the Holy Ghost. Her
experience was not of the rapturous character, but it was full of solid peace and
blessed, purifying hope, through the Divine
mercy. She was a *noble woman.* I do not
think I ever heard her say an unkind word
of an absent person, or ever saw her moved
by an unholy temper."

Mrs. Shaw possessed a catholic spirit,
and evinced an interest in all that belonged
to the catholic Church, working in connection with the Bible Society, the Dorcas
Society, etc., until her health failed. But she
was a Methodist, and her love to Methodism
was both ardent and intelligent. In days
of trial, when misunderstandings were rife,
and Societies were rent, and friends were
changed to foes, she mourned and prayed.

Among her manuscripts I find the following entries :—

"*September* 23*rd*, 1849. — I have been greatly pained on account of the disturbed state of our Connexion. It has so affected me as to prevent my taking my usual rest. Perhaps I entered too warmly into the subject, for I felt my peace to be at stake. I have besought the Lord to undertake for us. Those words of the Saviour, ' What is that to thee? follow thou Me ' have hushed my fears, and led me to determine to *say* as little as possible, but to *pray* for the prosperity of Zion. Great God, Whose power is infinite, save us from error and pride, cause Thy face to shine upon us, and give us peace !

"*April* 14*th*, 1850.—My mind is pained as I think of the injury being done to many souls and to the cause of God. For three nights I could not sleep. My spirit was greatly moved, and I felt constrained to pray for power to resist and overcome anger, and to watch the issues of my heart, and say, ' Set a watch, O Lord, before my mouth;

keep the door of my lips,' that I offend not ' with my tongue.'

"*April 28th.*—Many who once ran well and partook of our privileges, now never come near us ; and some who formerly helped, refuse to contribute anything to the blessed cause of Missions. Alas ! Alas ! "

"To — —. *January*, 1850.—The two following passages of Scripture have been much in my thoughts of late : ' Let this mind be in you, which was also in Christ Jesus, etc. ;' and ' If any man have not the Spirit of Christ, he is none of His.' Such words should lead all professing godliness to self-examination and deep searchings of heart. I must say that the spirit manifested in the late agitation has been a source of grief and pain to my mind. I deeply deplore the injurious effect both on sincere Christians, and on others who were disposed to unite with us, and seek redemption in the blood of Christ. It is to be feared that many such are turned out of the way ; and, should they perish, of whom will their blood be required ? . . . If the Word of Truth were made the rule of our life, it would bring peace to the conscience and be manifested in uniform consistency. See 1 Corinthians xiii.

" When you became a Wesleyan-Methodist, I presume it was a *voluntary* act. You knew the rules, or ought to have known them, and if any change of opinion cause you now to disapprove, you are quite at liberty to withdraw. No one constrains you to remain contrary to your judgment. . . . You must be fully aware that in every Christian Society it is of vital importance that the members should be united in love, in zeal and in effort to promote each other's welfare; and that envy, strife, fault-finding and contention must tend to destroy all that is good. While you profess to be a Methodist, and to love God, let it be seen that you ' adorn the doctrine of God our Saviour in all things,' by humbleness of mind, by meekness, by long-suffering, by esteeming others better than yourself, and especially by ' endeavouring to keep the unity of the Spirit in the bond of peace.' . . . O beware lest Satan get the advantage of you ! He is a subtle foe, long skilled in deceiving and destroying souls. Let me entreat you to stop and consider consequences. Pray mightily to Him Who is able to save. That He may vouchsafe to you the wisdom which cometh from above, grace to serve Him acceptably, and finally, eternal life, is the sincere desire of

"Your aged Friend,
"E. S."

It must not be supposed that because Mrs. Shaw wrote thus she could see no defects in the *working* of Methodism, or believed that improvement was impossible. On the contrary, she sometimes saw what she thought wrong, and mentioned it; but she believed that those wrongs were in general to be set right by *keeping* the rules rather than by *mending* them. The financial state of the Circuit with which she was connected during the latter years of her life, at times gave her anxiety. She regarded quarterly deficiencies and Circuit debts as hindrances to prosperity; and, that she was acquainted with the best means for preventing these evils, the following paper plainly shows. It would be well if the rule to which she refers were attended to in every Society and in every Class.

"Being an old member of the Wesleyan Society, I feel deeply concerned for the prosperity of Zion; and in my opinion nothing would tend so much to the comfort and happiness of all as strict adherence to our original rules. As honest men and women who have had the opportunity of hearing and reading those rules, and who have voluntarily become members of the Society, it seems to me that we are *bound* to conform to them. I would refer especially to the *weekly payments* in our Classes, which in many instances have been sadly neglected. Perhaps some, from inconsideration, from long habit or from prejudice, may feel an objection to lay aside their old practice and act upon this recommendation; but only let the trial be made for one or two quarters, and I believe the good effect would be seen in the relief of the Societies and Circuit from those embarrassments which have occasioned so much unpleasant feeling

in our Quarterly Meetings, injurious alike
to ministers and people. Ought we not to
resolve, one and all, to set out anew? Let
us 'love one another with a pure heart fervently,' and esteem our ministers 'very
highly in love for their work's sake; and
be at peace among ourselves.' "

CHAPTER XIV.

WAITING.

In the spring of 1853, after a residence of twenty-one years at St. Austell, Mr. and Mrs. Shaw removed to the sea-side village of Charlestown, where in retirement and comfort the aged couple patiently waited for the Master's coming.

Though Mrs. Shaw had now attained her eightieth year, she continued, as far as her failing strength would admit, to exert herself in the cause of God; and she still manifested an unabated interest in whatever affected the public weal, or the prosperity of the Church of Christ. The diary was not forgotten. Passing events, family changes and her experience of God's continued love were duly recorded; and not until the year 1865 did she lay aside her pen. With notices of the death of her husband, and the sudden removal of her son-in-law, the Rev. Joseph Entwisle, from the house of prayer to the mansions of light, the journal ends : an affecting close. It seemed as if now she could write no more. From the latter pages I take the following extracts :—

" *October* 17*th*, 1852.—Through the goodness and mercy of God I have enjoyed much peace and freedom from anxious care. I have prayed to be directed aright by the counsel of my best friends, and that our minds may be influenced according to His will Who cannot err. The cloud appears to me to rise, and I wish to follow. Though our contemplated plan is one which I have for years secretly wished for, yet I would not obstinately follow my own will if others disapprove, as I am conscious of ignorance and blindness in various respects, and I know not what will be best. O Lord, do Thou direct our steps ! Blessed be God, I feel my soul aspiring heavenward, and I long to enjoy more of the quickening, sanctifying influences of the Holy Spirit. An expression in Mr. Greeves' sermon to-day afforded me much comfort : ' Notwithstanding our multiplied sins and transgressions, the mercies of God are greater than they.'

"*January* 9*th*, 1853.—I thank God for His tender care and sparing mercy, and that I am permitted to see the beginning of another year with renewed bodily health, though with increased inability to walk. Monday last was the sixty-eighth anniversary of the day when I received a note of admission into the Methodist Society from the late Dr. Adam Clarke, then a young man in this Circuit. O the long-suffering of God towards me an ' unprofitable servant '! The thought is very humbling, that, notwithstanding such multiplied mercies, I have been so unfruitful.

"Prospect Cottage, Charlestown, *June* 19*th*, 1853.—Every day's enjoyment of this peaceful, lovely spot increases our grateful praises to Him Who has so graciously and wonderfully directed our steps hither. O that I may ever live in the spirit of entire dependence on God ! He careth for us.

" *February 5th*, 1854.—I have lately felt increasing desires for holiness in all its heights and depths, and a full meetness for the heavenly rest. Notwithstanding these desires, I am not always so devotional as to keep heaven in view. I feel Satan is still the accuser, and suggests unbelieving fears. In reading the second edition of Mr. Entwisle's Memoirs, and perceiving that he himself, with many of the excellent ones of the earth, have had their dark and cloudy seasons, I have been greatly encouraged to hope in God when cast down through temptation.

" *April* 23rd.—On Wednesday last I was permitted to close eighty-one years of my pilgrimage on earth. In the morning I felt more than usually the spirit of praise and devotion. It was truly good to wait upon God.

" *April* 30th.—Wednesday was the day appointed for humiliation and prayer because of the war. It was a day to be remembered. O that God may arise and get to Himself the victory, and cause ' the wrath of man ' to praise Him!

" *Good Friday, April 6th,* 1855.—Daily do I praise my good and gracious God for temporal mercies, and above all for power to trust and not be afraid. I feel the outward man decaying, and secret intimations that the time is short. O I long to be ready, and to say from my heart,

'No cross, no suffering I decline,
Only let all my heart be Thine'!

Lord, strengthen me to bear the answer!

"*Christmas-day,* 1855.—Sometimes clouds have seemed to hide the beams of the Sun of Righteousness: at other times the Word of God has been very precious. The text 'For Thou, Lord, art good, and ready to forgive; and plenteous in mercy unto all them that call upon Thee,' has afforded me much encouragement. Both my dear husband and I have many infirmities. Old age is not desirable. O that our mental powers may be continued to us in their full exercise, and our life of mercies crowned with a safe and peaceful, if not triumphant end!

"*August 3rd,* 1856.—To the praise and

glory of my Heavenly Father I am permitted to record with a grateful heart that during the past week I have been favoured with freedom from doubts and fears, and have enjoyed a clearer sense of the compassion and love of God in the unspeakable gift of His Son. I have prayed 'Father, glorify Thy Son in my salvation and deliverance from fears and doubts, and give me the full assurance of faith and a still greater hungering and thirsting after righteousness.' We had a good season at the Class-meeting this afternoon.

"*October* 12*th.*—O how shall I praise my gracious, long-suffering God for His supporting, sustaining grace, and for His precious Word!

"*Good Friday, April* 10*th,* 1857.—To-day my heart has been cheered while meditating on the amazing love of God to a lost and fallen world. And if He so loved me as to die for me, surely He is both able and willing to save to the *uttermost!*

"*August* 16*th.*—I would gratefully adore my Heavenly Father for His multiplied mercies. The beautiful weather for harvest

P

causes me to feel thankful. While the Conference has been assembled I have been drawn out to pray that the great Head of the Church may eminently preside among His servants, direct all their plans and appoint them to stations where their labours may be most useful and their example most beneficial.

" *October* 11*th.*—On 29th ult. and 1st inst. I was favoured with such a manifestation of the goodness, mercy and love of God in all His dispensations towards me from early youth to the present, that it seemed that I had not a wish or desire for anything; but that all my wants were supplied. O what a fulness did I feel in Him! Truly *God is love.* Sunday was a good day. I felt not only ' peace,' but ' joy in the Holy Ghost.' O may I ever be enabled to say, ' Thy will be done' !

" *January* 3*rd,* 1858.—Varied feelings have occupied my heart this morning. Seventy-three years ago, to-day, I received my note of admittance into the Methodist Society from the Rev. Adam Clarke. What shall I say ? ' Enter not into judgment with

Thy servant,' O Lord, because of unfaithfulness, forgetfulness and innumerable shortcomings, and deepen my feelings of grateful praise for Thy great goodness. I look back on the days of my childhood and youth, and exclaim,—

> 'O the infinite cares, And temptations, and snares,
>   Thy hand hath conducted me through!
> O the blessings bestow'd By a bountiful God,
>   And the mercies eternally new!'

For a long time after I began to meet in Class I was destitute of clear perceptions of the way of salvation. My determination was

> 'If I ne'er find the sacred road,
>   I'll perish crying out for God.'

I fasted, wept, prayed and used much self-denial in eating, in apparel, in sleeping, and in everything which I thought inconsistent with a life of entire consecration to God. After some years, while conversing with that excellent man, the late Rev. Francis Truscott, I was encouraged and enabled to lay hold on Jesus as my atoning

Saviour, and to believe that I was accepted through His precious sacrifice. Thenceforward I have held on my way without a temptation to turn back to the 'beggarly elements' of the world, sometimes weak and 'faint, yet pursuing.' And now that I am near the end of my race, I have, I trust, a well-grounded hope of eternal life through our Lord and Saviour Jesus Christ.

"*March* 21st.—On the 16th ult. dear Augustus Rogers * most peacefully entered into eternal rest. Notwithstanding severe sufferings, no murmur or complaint escaped his lips. After last Christmas-day, when he experienced a blessed manifestation of the love of Christ at the sacrament of the Lord's Supper, he seemed to enjoy perfect peace.

"*October* 17th.—On the 5th inst. I received a letter from America, written by a friend, at the request of my dear Samuel, who was unable to write himself, except an

---

* Another son of the Rev. Thomas Rogers, and brother of Robert, whose death, in 1848, is referred to on a previous page.

almost illegible scrawl at the conclusion. 'Farewell, dear Mother,' he wrote, 'I hope, through the merits of Jesus, to meet you in heaven.' The contents of the letter left very little doubt of his removal to a better world. This, though not quite unexpected, caused tears of natural sorrow.

"*October* 31*st.*—This morning I have felt so much gratitude and praise to my Heavenly Father that He has taken to Himself my dear Samuel as I cannot express. O how often have my fears and anxieties painfully oppressed me when thinking of his temptations, privations and various afflictions, and without the least hope of ever seeing me again! Now he is for ever safe; saved of the Lord, in heaven, beholding His glory and uniting in the song of the redeemed.

"*April* 19*th,* 1863.—I want to feel more ardent love to God, a greater delight in prayer and a fuller assurance that I am right. O how manifold have been the mercies bestowed on me, and in how many instances has the Lord been better to me than all my fears! My dear husband is quite deaf. What a mercy it would be if

God were pleased to take us together to heaven! This is the ninetieth anniversary of my birthday.

"*Good Friday*, 1864. — On Sunday, May 17th, 1863, I heard my dear husband praying most fervently that God would pardon all that he had ever done or said amiss, that He would fully prepare him for His kingdom, and give him an easy death. As was frequently the case he repeated some of his favourite hymns,—

'O for a heart to praise my God! etc.';

'A charge to keep I have, etc.';

'Now I have found the ground wherein, etc.'

He was in a very happy frame of mind, and continued so until he retired to rest. On the following morning as he sat in his chair, he sank into a deep sleep, and awoke no more. He was ninety-seven years of age. His remains were carried to the grave on the following Saturday morning. When all was over, and I had time to reflect on the goodness and mercy of my Heavenly Father in fully preparing, and taking him first, as he was unable to dress himself, and I, though feeble, was enabled to assist him daily, I could not help saying, 'He hath done all things well;' and I now desire to 'praise Him for all that is past, and trust Him for all that's to come.' God has graciously visited my soul, and given me to feel that 'the blood of Jesus Christ cleanseth from all sin;' and, though Satan assaults me with doubts and fears, yet He who knows all things, knows that I love Him, and would not willingly grieve Him.

"*August* 23*rd*, 1864.—I am recovering from a severe illness, but it has been a sanctified affliction. I have felt some little increase of faith and love, and my confidence has been strengthened on calling to remembrance former mercies and answers to prayer.

"*December* 11*th*, 1864.—I am permitted to resume my pen to record mercies and trials. I feel the increasing infirmities of old age; and the unexpected and painful announcement by last night's post of the sudden departure of my excellent son-in-law, Joseph Entwisle, has greatly affected me. He was giving out the verse beginning 'God moves in a mysterious way,' in the chapel at

Moorside, in the Yeadon Circuit, when he sank back in the pulpit and expired :—

> His body with his charge laid down,
> And ceased at once to work and live.

He died on the 8th.   Just eighty-two years since my own dear mother died, leaving me, as she said, 'in the Lord's hand,' Who, she doubted not, would take care of me. . . . O my Heavenly Father, sanctify this trial to me and all the dear relatives, and bless me with a full meetness for Thy kingdom!"

The journal terminates with the brief but comprehensive prayer, "O Lord, do Thou help me to trust in Thee!" And that prayer was answered.

The seven remaining years of Mrs. Shaw's stay upon earth, though years of feebleness, were characterised, as by-gone years had been, by cheerful resignation and almost unbroken peace.   "I do not wish to live to old age: it is not desirable," she had said in her younger days, as she noted the querulousness, childishness and dissatisfaction which are often the companions of the aged. Mrs. Shaw never changed that opinion; but when she herself became old a cheerful spirit, deep humility and thankfulness made her last years beautiful. They were as the mellow autumn which follows the rich and glorious summer, or as the bright, calm evening which succeeds the hot and busy day. Looking back upon an active life consecrated to Him her soul loved, and still sustained by Divine grace, she moved peacefully onward to the grave, and to the brightness which, by the eye of faith, she saw beyond it. She had Jesus with her, and He made " the age venerable, and the weakness dignified, and the dying-bed beautiful, and the last departure blessed, and the terrible funeral ' a door opened in heaven.' " *

* Dr. C. J. Vaughan.

CHAPTER XV.

"*FOR EVER WITH THE LORD.*"

DURING three years' residence in St. Austell (1868—1871) it was the writer's happiness to pay frequent visits to our venerable friend. At times she was bright and communicative ; at other times she appeared somewhat absent, and unable to call up the remembrance of what had taken place but a little while before. But at *all* times she had a hearty welcome for her visitor, and she never tired when talking of the love of Jesus, and the state of the Work of God. As she narrated some of the incidents of her childhood and youth, or made shrewd remarks in reference to more recent events, or told of God's dealings with her during " the days of the years of her pilgrimage," a smile would play upon her counte-

nance, and such was her buoyancy of spirit
that it seemed hard to realise the fact that
she was verging on her hundredth year.

In attire she was a good representative of
the aged Methodists of more than fifty
years ago. She saw no need for following—
she felt no inclination to follow—the ever-
changing fashions of these latter days, and
she deplored the increasing rage for that
"outward adorning" which undoubtedly
in many cases proves a hindrance to the
growth of religion in the soul. No one
looking at her in her mob-cap, quaker-like
bonnet and neat shawl, would have been
likely to suppose that love of dress had ever
been with her a "besetting" sin.

In extreme old age the spirit of liberality,
and the desire to relieve the wants of the
poor, which, as we have seen, were promi-
nent characteristics in early days, were still
manifest. The poverty-stricken and the
sick were remembered by her, and, not
content with supplying them herself, she
sought to induce others to take an interest
in their case, and relieve them too. When
school-rooms were being erected in con-

nection with the Wesleyan chapel at Charlestown, she was ready to do all that lay in her power to help on the good work ; and it is worthy of record that, while she gave according to her ability, she also disposed of several of her earliest Society tickets to some collector of Methodist antiquities, and handed the proceeds of the sale to the Treasurer of the Building Fund.

When her sight had become very defective,—indeed, almost to the last,—Mrs. Shaw continued her correspondence. She wrote when she could not see to read what she had written ; and it is affecting to note the contrast between the penmanship of her first letters and that of her last. More touching still is it to observe indications of failing memory and the loss of mental vigour. And yet, her age being considered, the last letters she wrote are marvellously correct. I append a few extracts from some that have fallen into my hands.

To Mrs. Eacott.

"*February* 20*th*, 1868.

" My dearest Emily,—

" I am become a very poor corre-
spondent. . . . My sight is dim, and my
hearing is dull; but I am surrounded with
mercies. I am free from strong pain;
although inflammatory attacks remind me
that here I have 'no continuing city.' I am,
through the tender mercy of my Heavenly
Father, preserved from condemnation, and
I long to feel at all times a full meetness
for the glorious inheritance above. When
I consider my great age, I feel very thankful that I possess soundness of mind, and
that I am able to read when the light is
good, and the print not very small; and to
write, though seldom able to read what I
have written. . . ."

To the same.

"*October* 11*th*, 1869.

". . . Through the tender mercies of our
Heavenly Father, I am quite as well as I

can expect to be at my advanced age (ninety-seven). I am very feeble, not able to rise from my chair or to sit down without help. . . . May you be led in the path appointed by our God, where you may be engaged in doing and in getting good. Though I have not written to you lately, I do not forget you. I pray that the richest blessing of our Almighty Saviour may rest on you and your beloved husband."

To the same.
"*August 5th,* 1871.

" . . . Although I am become very forgetful of almost every one and every thing, I do not forget to pray that a full meetness for the glorious inheritance may be vouchsafed to myself, and all my beloved relatives and friends. Our Mr. Barratt is now at the Conference from this Circuit; and if you see him he can tell you more than I can see to write."

To the Rev. R. C. Barratt.
"*July,* 1869.

" When I saw you yesterday, you told me

of your intention to go to the Conference this year. As there are many of the preachers whom I highly esteem, who may possibly remember me as an old member, and now being in my ninety-seventh year since the 19th of last April, I will beg the favour of your presenting my affectionate respects to any who may inquire for me, and tell them that I have proved God to be faithful to all His promises. He graciously protects and preserves me. He keeps my mind in peace, and gives me to taste His love; and I have a good hope of everlasting life through the atonement and intercession of our glorious Redeemer. May the Divine presence overshadow the Assembly when they meet, direct all their steps, and ever crown them with His blessing!"

To Mr. and Mrs. John Shaw.

" *April 8th,* 1871.

" . . . On taking a review of the past, I am constrained to acknowledge that all has been for my good. O ' trust in the Lord for ever, for in the Lord Jehovah is everlasting strength!' He doeth ' all things well,' as

you will see when you draw so near the end
of the race as I am.　May we be more and
more convinced of this, love Him with all
our heart, mind, soul and strength, and
finally praise Him for ever and ever."

To the same.

"*May* 23*rd*, 1871.

" This is my first attempt to write a short
note after a time of weakness and indisposition.　Through the tender mercy of God I
have passed another anniversary of my
birthday.

' Be they many or few, My days are His due,
　And they all are devoted to Him.'

Should you be able to spend a day or two
here, I shall be glad to see you once more
before I leave this world of shadows to go
to our Father's house above, where we shall
know no separation, and enjoy glory everlasting.　Amen.　Accept my best love, and
believe me to remain

"Your affectionate mother,
"Elizabeth Shaw,
"(*now in her ninety-ninth year.*)"

In the early part of the year 1872, it was apparent that Mrs. Shaw was drawing very near to the end of her life's long day ; and " at eventide " it was " light." There were times when the great adversary powerfully assaulted her ; but the sword of the Spirit, that trusty weapon with which she had fought so many fights, and won so many victories, did not fail her at the last. As she dwelt on the precious promises, and exercised faith in the all-sufficient Atonement, and looked forward to the bright heaven, now so near, she experienced "peace and joy in the Holy Ghost."

" One morning about a week before her decease," writes Mr. John Shaw, " we were favoured with a most solemn and blessed season in prayer together. It was indeed ' fellowship with the Father, and with His Son Jesus Christ.' We were admitted into the Holy of Holies by the ' new and living way ;' and we felt that we had ' come unto Mount Sion, and unto the city of the living God, the heavenly Jerusalem, and to an innumerable company of angels, to the general assembly and Church of the firstborn,

Q

which are written in heaven, and to God
the Judge of all, and to the spirits of just
men made perfect, and to Jesus the Media-
tor of the New Covenant, and to the blood
of sprinkling, that speaketh better things
than that of Abel.' On rising from my
knees, I noticed that her eyes were beautifully bright, and that her countenance
appeared radiant with the divine peace and
heavenly hope which she felt within. Lift-
ing her eyes and hands towards heaven, with
peculiar pathos she exclaimed,—

' Me for Thine own Thou lov'st to take,
   In time and in eternity :
Thou never, never wilt forsake
   A helpless worm that trusts in Thee !' "

And so the aged saint waited for her
dismissal until, on the 9th of March, 1872,
she heard her Saviour say, " Enter thou into
the joy of thy Lord," and fell asleep, aged
ninety-nine years.

" Devout men carried " her to her
" burial." In accordance with her own wish,
eight Local-preachers were chosen as bearers,
to each of whom was given a copy of the
New Testament, which she had provided for

the purpose a few years before her death. In the church-yard at Charlestown, awaiting the resurrection to eternal life, her remains were laid in the same grave with those of her departed husband.

Thus lived and died "a mother in Israel." Be it ours to follow her as she followed Christ, and so when we leave "this world of shadows" we shall join her in "our Father's house above."